Elsie Inglis / The Woman with the 7

Eva Shaw McLaren

PREFACE

"To light a path for men to come" is the privilege of the pioneer; and the life of a pioneer, the hewer of a new path, is always encouraging, whether he who goes before to open the way be a voyager to the Poles or the uttermost parts of the earth, in imminent danger of physical death, or whether he be an adventurer, cutting a path to a new race consciousness, revealing the power of service in new vocations, evoking new powers, and living in hourly danger of mental suffocation by prejudices and inhibitions of race tradition.

The women's irresistible movement, which has so suddenly flooded all departments of work previously considered the monopoly of men, required from the leaders indomitable courage, selflessness, and faith, qualities of imperishable splendour; and to read the life of Elsie Inglis is to recognize instantly that she was one of these ruthless adventurers, hewing her way through all perils and difficulties to bring to pass the dreams of thousands of women. The world's standard of success may appear to give the prize to those who collect things, but in reality the crown of victory, the laurel wreath, the tribute beyond all material value, is always reserved for those invisible, intangible qualities which are evinced in character.

It is wonderful to read how slowly and surely that character was formed through twenty years of monotonous routine. The establishing of a Hospice for women and children, run entirely by women, was not a popular movement, and through long years of dull, arduous work, patient, silent, honest, dedicated unconsciously to the service of others, she laid the foundations which led to her great achievement, and so, full of courage and growing in power, like Nelson she developed a blind eye, to which she put her telescope in times of bewilderment; she could never see the difficulties which loomed large in her way—sex prejudices and mountains of race convictions to be moved—and so she moved them!

In founding The Hospice she gave herself first to the women and children round her; later, in the urgent call of the Suffrage movement, she

3

devoted herself whole-heartedly to the service of the women of the country, and so she was ready when the war came. Her own country refused her services; but Providence has a strange way of turning what appears to be evil into great good. The refusal of the British Government to accept the services of medically trained women caused them to offer their services elsewhere; and so she went first to help the French, and then to encourage and serve Serbia in her dire need.

And so from the first she was a pioneer: in doing medical work among women and children; in achieving the rights of citizenship for women; and in the further great adventure of establishing the true League of Nations which lies in the will to serve mankind.

LENA ASHWELL

(Mrs. Henry Simson)

INTRODUCTION

A most interesting *Life* of Elsie Inglis, written a short time ago by the Lady Frances Balfour, has had a wide circulation which has proved the appreciation of the public.

This second *Life* appears at the request of The Society for Promoting Christian Knowledge that I should write a short memoir of my sister, to be included in the "Pioneers of Progress" Series which it is publishing. I undertake the duty with joy.

In accordance with the series in which it appears, the *Life* is a short one, but it has been possible to incorporate in it some fresh material. Not the least interesting is what has been taken from the manuscript of a novel by Dr. Inglis, found amongst her papers some time after her death. It is called *The Story of a Modern Woman*. It was probably written between the years 1906 and 1914; the outbreak of the war may have prevented its publication. The date given in the first chapter of the story is 1904. Very evidently the book expresses Elsie Inglis's views on life. Quotations have been made from it, as it gives an insight into her own character and experiences.

The endeavour has been made to draw a picture of her as she appeared to those who knew her best. She was certainly a fine character, full of life and movement, ever growing and developing, ever glorying in new adventure. There was no stagnation about Elsie Inglis. Independent, strong, keen (if sometimes impatient), and generous, from her childhood she was ever a great giver.

Alongside all the energy and force in her character there were great depths of tenderness. "Nothing like sitting on the floor for half an hour playing with little children to prepare you for a strenuous bit of work," was one of her sayings.

Not to many women, perhaps, have other women given such a wealth of love as they gave to Elsie Inglis. In innumerable letters received after her death is traceable the idea expressed by one woman: "In all your sorrow, remember, I loved her too."

Those who worked with her point again and again to a characteristic that distinguished her all her life—her complete disregard of the opinion of others about herself personally, while she pursued the course her conscience dictated, and yet she drew to herself the affectionate regard of many who knew her for the first time during the last three years of her life.

What her own countrymen thought of her will be found in the pages of this book, but the touching testimony of a Serb and a Russian may be given here. A Serb orderly expressed his devotion in a way that Dr. Inglis used to recall with a smile: "Missis Doctor, I love you better than my mother, and my wife, and my family. Missis Doctor, I will never leave you."

And a soldier from Russia said of her: "She was loved amongst us as a queen, and respected as a saint."

"In her *Life* you want the testimony of those who saw *her*. Dr. Inglis's work before and during the war will find its place in any enduring record; what you want to impress on the minds of the succeeding generation is *the quality of the woman* of which that work was the final expression."

Something of what that quality was appears, it is hoped, in the pages of this memoir. I am grateful to men and women of varied outlook, who knew her at different periods of her life, for memories which have been drawn upon in this effort to picture Elsie Inglis.

EVA SHAW McLAREN

ELSIE INGLIS

Chapter I

ELSIE INGLIS

The War.

"Elsie Inglis was one of the heroic figures of the war."[1]

Suffrage.

"During the whole years of the Suffrage struggle, while the National Union of Women's Suffrage Societies was growing and developing, Dr. Elsie Inglis stood as a tower of strength, and her unbounded energy and unfailing courage helped the cause forward in more ways than she knew. To the London Society she stood out as a supporter of wise councils and bold measures; time after time, in the decisions of the Union, they found themselves by her side, and from England to Scotland they learned to look to her as to a staunch friend.

"Later, when the war transformed the work of the Societies of the Union, they trusted and followed her still, and it is their comfort now to think that in all her time of need it was their privilege to support her."[2]

Medical.

"We medical women in Scotland will miss her very much, for she was indeed a strong rock amongst us all."[3]

Scottish Women's Hospitals.

"Those who work in the hospitals she founded and for the Units she commanded, and all who witnessed her labours, feel inspired by her dauntless example. The character of the Happy Warrior was in some measure her

character. We reverence her calm fearlessness and forceful energies, her genius for overcoming obstacles, her common sense, her largeness of mind and purpose, and we rejoice in the splendour of her achievements."[4]
Home.

"It is not of her great qualities that I think now, but rather that she was such a darling."[5]
Serbia.

"By her knowledge she cured the physical wounds of the Serb soldiers. By her shining face she cured their souls. Silent, busy, smiling—that was her method. She strengthened the faith of her patients in *knowledge* and in *Christianity*. Scotland hardly could send to Serbia a better Christian missionary."[6]

As the days pass, bringing the figure of Elsie Inglis into perspective, these true and beautiful pictures of her fall quietly into the background, and one idea begins slowly to emerge and to expand, and to become the most real fact about her. As we follow her outward life and read the writings she left behind her, we come to realize that her greatness lay not so much in the things she achieved as in the hidden power of her spirit. *She was a woman of solved problems.* The far-reaching qualities of her mind and character are but the outcome of this inward condition.

All men and women have problems; few solve them. The solved problem in any life is the expression of genius, and is the cause of strength and peace in the character.

"It is amazing how sometimes a name begins to shine like a star, and then to glow and glow until it fills the firmament. Such a name is Elsie Inglis."[7]
FOOTNOTES:

9

[1] Dr. Seton-Watson.

[2] The London Committee of the N.U.W.S.S.

[3] A medical colleague.

[4] Mrs. Flinders Petrie.

[5] I. A. W., niece.

[6] Bishop Nicolai Velimirovic.

[7] Rev. Norman Maclean, D.D.

Chapter II

THE ROCK FROM WHICH SHE WAS HEWN

"It is not the weariness of mortality, but the Strength of Divinity which we have to recognize in all mighty things."

In the centre stands Elsie Inglis, the "woman of gentle breeding, short of stature, alert, and with the eyes of a seer," and "a smile like sunshine"; and on either side and behind this central figure the stage is crowded with men and women of long ago, the people of her race. One by one they catch our eye, and we note their connection with the central figure.

Far back in the group (for it is near two hundred years ago) stands Hugh Inglis, hailing from Inverness-shire. He was a loyal supporter of Prince Charlie, and the owner of a yacht, which he used in gun-running in the service of the Prince.

A little nearer are two of Elsie's great-grandfathers, John Fendall and Alexander Inglis. John Fendall was Governor of Java at the time when the island was restored to the Dutch. The Dutch fleet arrived to take it over before Fendall had received his instructions from the Government, and he refused to give it up till they reached him—a gesture not without a parallel in the later years of the life of his descendant. Alexander Inglis, leaving Inverness-shire, emigrated to South Carolina, and was there killed in a duel fought on some point of honour. Through his wife, Mary Deas, Elsie's descent runs up to Robert the Bruce on the one hand, and, on the other, to a family who left France after the revocation of the Edict of Nantes, and settled in Scotland.

As we thread our way through the various figures on the stage we are attracted by a group of three women. They are the daughters of the Governor of Java, "the three Miss Fendalls." One of them, Harriet, is Elsie's grandmother. All three married, and their descendants in the second generation numbered well over a hundred! Harriet Fendall married George Powney Thompson, whose father was at one time secretary to Warren

Hastings. George Thompson himself was a member of the East India Company, and ruled over large provinces in India. One of their nine daughters, Harriet Thompson, was Elsie's mother.

On the other side of the stage, in the same generation as the Miss Fendalls, is another group of women. These are the three sisters of Elsie's grandfather, David Inglis, son of Alexander, who fared forth to South Carolina, and counted honour more dear than life.

David was evidently a restless, keen, adventurous man; many years of his life were spent in India in the service of the East India Company. Of his three sisters—Katherine, painted by Raeburn; Mary, gentle and quiet; and Elizabeth—we linger longest near Elizabeth. She never married, and was an outstanding personality in the little family. She was evidently conversant with all the questions of the day, and commented on them in the long, closely written letters which have been preserved.

After David's return from India he must have intended at one time to stand for Parliament. Elizabeth writes to him from her "far corner" in Inverness-shire, giving him stirring advice, and demanding from him an uncompromising, high standard. She tells him to "unfurl his banner"; she knows "he will carry his religion into his politics." "Separate religion from politics!" cries Elizabeth; "as well talk of separating our every duty from religion!"

Needless anxiety, one would think, on the part of the good Highland lady, for the temptation to leave religion out of any of his activities can scarcely have assailed David. We read that when Elsie's grandfather had returned from the East to England he used to give missionary addresses, not, one would think, a common form of activity in a retired servant of the East India Company. One hears this note of genuine religion in the lives of those forebears of Elsie's.

THE MISSES FENDALL

Lady D'Oyly   **Mrs. Lowis**   **Mrs. Thompson**
                                         (Elsie's Grandmother)

THE MISSES FENDALL

FROM A DRAWING IN THE POSSESSION OF BRIGADIER-GENERAL C. FENDALL, C.B., C.M.G., D.S.O., ETC.

"The extraordinary thing in all the letters, whether they were written by an Inglis, a Deas, or a Money, is the pervading note of strong religious faith. They not only refer to religion, but often, in truly Scottish fashion, they enter on long theological dissertations."

David married Martha Money. Close to Martha on the stage stands her brother, William Taylor Money, Elsie's great-uncle. We greet him gladly, for he was a man of character. He was a friend of Wilberforce, and a Member of Parliament when the Anti-Slavery Bill was passed. Afterwards "he owned a merchant vessel, and gained great honour by his capture of several of the Dutch fleet, who mistook him for a British man-of-war, the smart appearance of his vessel with its manned guns deceiving them." There is a picture in Trinity House of his vessel bringing in the Dutch ships. Later, he was Consul-General at Venice and the north of Italy, where he died, in 1834, in his gondola! He had strong religious convictions, and would never infringe the sacredness of the Sabbath-day by any "secular work." In a short biography of him, written in 1835, the weight of his religious beliefs, which made themselves felt both in Parliament and when Consul, is dwelt on at length. A son of David and Martha Inglis, John Forbes David Inglis, was Elsie's father. John went to India in 1840, following his father's footsteps in the service of the East India Company. Thirty-six years of his life were spent there, with only one short furlough home. He rose to distinction in the service, and gained the love and trust of the Indian peoples. After he retired in 1876 one of his Indian friends addressed a letter to him, "John Inglis, England, Tasmania, or wherever else he may be, this shall be delivered to him," and through the ingenuity of the British Post Office it was delivered in Tasmania.

Elsie's mother, Harriet Thompson, went out to India when she was seventeen to her father, George Powney Thompson. She married when she was eighteen.

She met her future husband, John Inglis, at a dance in her father's house. Her children were often told by their father of the white muslin dress, with large purple flowers all over it, worn by her that evening, and how he and several of his friends, young men in the district, drove fifty miles to have the chance of dancing with her!

"She must have had a steady nerve, for her letters are full of various adventures in camp and tiger-haunted jungles, and most of them narrate the presence of one of her infants, who was accompanying the parents on their routine of Indian official life." In 1858, when John Inglis was coming home on his one short furlough, she trekked down from Lahore to Calcutta with the six children in country conveyances. The journey took four months; then came the voyage round the Cape, another four months. Of course she had the help of ayahs and bearers on the journeys, but even with such help it was no easy task.

John Inglis saw his family settled in Southampton, and almost immediately had to return to India, on the outbreak of the Mutiny. His wife stayed at home with the children, until India was again a safe place for English women, when she rejoined her husband in 1863.

They crowd round Elsie Inglis, these men and women in their quaint and attractive costumes of long ago; we feel their influence on her; we see their spirit mingling with hers. As we run our eye over the crowded stage, we see the dim outline of the rock from which she was hewn, we feel the spirit which was hers, and we hail it again as it drives her forth to play her part in the great drama of the last three years of her life.

The members of every family, every group of blood relations, are held together by the unseen spirit of their generations. It matters little whether they can trace their descent or not; the peculiar spirit of that race which is theirs fashions them for particular purposes and work. And what are they all but the varied expressions of the One Divine Mind, of the Endless Life of God?

ELSIE INGLIS AT THE AGE OF 2 YEARS

ELSIE INGLIS

AT THE AGE OF 2 YEARS

Chapter III

1864—1894

Elsie Inglis was born on August 16, 1864, in India. The wide plains of India, the "huddled hills" and valleys of the Himalayas, were the environment with which Nature surrounded her for the first twelve years of her life. Her childhood was a happy one, and the most perfect friendship existed between her and her father from her earliest days.

"All our childhood is full of remembrances of father.[8] He never forgot our birthdays; however hot it was down in the scorched plains, when the day came round, if we were up in the hills, a large parcel would arrive from him. His very presence was joy and strength when he came to us at Naini Tal. What a remembrance there is of early breakfasts and early walks with him—the father and the three children! The table was spread in the verandah between six and seven. Father made three cups of cocoa, one for each of us, and then the glorious walk! The ponies followed behind, each with their attendant grooms, and two or three red-coated chaprassies, father stopping all along the road to talk to every native who wished to speak to him, while we three ran about, laughing and interested in everything. Then, at night, the shouting for him after we were in bed, and father's step bounding up the stair in Calcutta, or coming along the matted floor of our hill home. All order and quietness were flung to the winds while he said good-night to us.

"It was always understood that Elsie and he were special chums, but that never made any jealousy. Father was always just. The three cups of cocoa were always the same in quantity and quality. We got equal shares of his right and his left hand in our walks; but Elsie and he were comrades, inseparables from the day of her birth.

"In the background of our lives there was always the quiet, strong mother, whose eyes and smile live on through the years. Every morning before the breakfast and walk there were five minutes when we sat in front of her in a row on little chairs in her room and read the Scripture verses in turn,

16

and then knelt in a straight, quiet row and repeated the prayers after her. Only once can I remember father being angry with any of us, and that was when one of us ventured to hesitate in instant obedience to some wish of hers. I still see the room in which it happened, and the thunder in his voice is with me still."

There was a constant change of scene during these years in India—Allahabad, Naini Tal, Calcutta, Simla, and Lucknow. After her father retired, two years in Australia visiting older brothers who had settled there, and then in 1878 home to the land of her fathers.

On the voyage home, when Elsie was about fourteen, her mother writes of her:

"Elsie has found occupation for herself in helping to nurse sick children and look after turbulent boys who trouble everybody on board, and a baby of seven months old is an especial favourite with her."

But through the changing scenes there was always growing and deepening the beautiful comradeship between father and daughter. The family settled in Edinburgh, and Elsie went to school to the Charlotte Square Institution, perhaps in those days the best school for girls in Edinburgh. In the history class taught by Mr. Hossack she was nearly always at the top.

Of her school life in Edinburgh a companion writes:

"I remember quite distinctly when the girls of 23, Charlotte Square were told that two girls from Tasmania were coming to the school, and a certain feeling of surprise that the said girls were just like ordinary mortals, though the big, earnest brows and the hair quaintly parted in the middle and done up in plaits fastened up at the back of the head were certainly not ordinary.

"A friend has the story of a question going round the class; she thinks Clive or Warren Hastings was the subject of the lesson, and the question was what one would do if a calumny were spread about one. 'Deny it,' one girl answered. 'Fight it,' another. Still the teacher went on asking. 'Live it down,' said Elsie. 'Right, Miss Inglis.' My friend writes: 'The question I cannot remember; it was the bright, confident smile with the answer, and Mr. Hossack's delighted wave to the top of the class that abides in my memory.'

"I always think a very characteristic story of Elsie is her asking that the school might have permission to play in Charlotte Square Gardens. In those days no one thought of providing fresh-air exercise for girls except by walks, and tennis was just coming in. Elsie had the courage (to us schoolgirls it seemed extraordinary courage) to confront the three Directors of the school, and ask if we might be allowed to play in the gardens of the Square. The three Directors together were to us the most formidable and awe-inspiring body, though separately they were amiable and estimable men!

"The answer was, we might play in the gardens if the residents of the Square would give their consent, and the heroic Elsie, with, I think, one other girl, actually went round to each house in the Square and asked consent of the owner. In those days the inhabitants of Charlotte Square were very select and exclusive indeed, and we all felt it was a brave thing to do. Elsie gained her point, and the girls played at certain hours in the Square till a regular playing-field was arranged.... Elsie's companion or companions in this first adventure to influence those in authority have been spoken of as 'her first Unit.'"[9]

When she was eighteen she went for a year to Paris with six other girls, in charge of Miss Gordon Brown. She came home again shortly before her mother's death in January, 1885. Henceforth she was her father's constant companion. They took long walks together, talked on every subject, and enjoyed many humorous episodes together. On one point only they disagreed—Home Rule for Ireland: she for it, he against.

During the nine years from 1885 to her father's death in 1894, she began and completed her medical studies with his full approval. The great fight for the opening of the door for women to study medicine had been fought and won earlier by Dr. Sophia Jex-Blake, Dr. Garrett Anderson, and others. But though the door was open, there was still much opposition to be encountered and a certain amount of persecution to be borne when the women of Dr. Inglis's time ventured to enter the halls of medical learning.

Along the pathway made easy for them by these women of the past, hundreds of young women are to-day entering the medical profession. As we look at them we realize that in their hands, to a very large extent, lies the solving of the acutest problem of our race—the relation of the sexes. Will they fail us? Will they be content with a solution along lines that can only be called a second best? When we remember the clear-brained women in whose steps they follow, who opened the medical world for them, and whose spirits will for ever overshadow the women who walk in it, we know they will not fail us.

Elsie Inglis pursued her medical studies in Edinburgh and Glasgow. After she qualified she was for six months House-Surgeon in the New Hospital for Women and Children in London, and then went to the Rotunda in Dublin for a few months' special study in midwifery.

She returned home in March, 1894, in time to be with her father during his last illness. Daily letters had passed between them whenever she was away from home. His outlook on life was so broad and tolerant, his judgment on men and affairs so sane and generous, his religion so vital, that with perfect truth she could say, as she did, at one of the biggest meetings she addressed after her return from Serbia: "If I have been able to do anything, I owe it all to my father."

After his death she started practice with Dr. Jessie Macgregor at 8, Walker Street, Edinburgh. It was a happy partnership for the few years it lasted, until for family reasons Dr. Macgregor left Scotland for America. Dr. Inglis stayed on in Walker Street, taking over Dr. Macgregor's practice. Then followed years of hard work and interests in many directions.

JOHN FORBES DAVID INGLIS, ELSIE INGLIS' FATHER

JOHN FORBES DAVID INGLIS

ELSIE INGLIS' FATHER

"If I have been able to do anything—whatever I am, whatever I have done—
I owe it all to my Father."

Elsie Inglis, at a meeting held in the Criterion
Theatre, London, April 5th, 1916

The Hospice for Women and Children in the High Street of Edinburgh was started. Her practice grew, and she became a keen suffragist. During these years also she evidently faced and solved her problems.

She was a woman capable of great friendships. During the twenty years of her professional life perhaps the three people who stood nearest to her were her sister, Mrs. Simson, and the Very Rev. Dr. and Mrs. Wallace Williamson. These friendships were a source of great strength and comfort to her.

We may fitly close this chapter by quoting descriptions of Dr. Inglis by two of her friends—Miss S. E. S. Mair, of Edinburgh, and Dr. Beatrice Russell:

"In outward appearance Dr. Inglis was no Amazon, but just a woman of gentle breeding, courteous, sweet-voiced, somewhat short of stature, alert, and with the eyes of a seer, blue-grey and clear, looking forth from under a brow wide and high, with soft brown hair brushed loosely back; with lips often parted in a radiant smile, discovering small white teeth and regular, but lips which were at times firmly closed with a fixity of purpose such as would warn off unwarrantable opposition or objections from less bold workers. Those clear eyes had a peculiar power of withdrawing on rare occasions, as it were, behind a curtain when their owner desired to absent herself from discussion of points on which she preferred to give no opinion. It was no mere expression such as absent-mindedness might produce, but was, as she herself was aware, a voluntary action of withdrawal from all participation in what was going on. The discussion over, in a moment the blinds would be up and the soul looked forth through its clear windows with steady gaze. Whether the aural doors had been closed also there is no knowing."

"She was a keen politician—in the pre-war days a staunch supporter of the Liberal party, and in the years immediately preceding the war she devoted much of her time to work in connection with the Women's Suffrage movement. She was instrumental in organizing the Scottish Federation of Women's Suffrage Societies, and was Honorary Secretary of the Federation up to the time of her death. But the factor which most greatly contributed to her influence was the unselfishness of her work. She truly 'set the cause above renown' and loved 'the game beyond the prize.' She was always above the suspicion of working for ulterior motives or grinding a personal axe. It was ever the work, and not her own share in it, which concerned her, and no one was more generous in recognizing the work of others.

"To her friends Elsie Inglis is a vivid memory, yet it is not easy clearly to put in words the many sides of her character. In the care of her patients she was sympathetic, strong, and unsparing of herself; in public life she was a good speaker and a keen fighter; while as a woman and a friend she was a delightful mixture of sound good sense, quick temper, and warm-hearted impulsiveness—a combination of qualities which won her many devoted friends. A very marked feature of her character was an unusual degree of optimism which never failed her. Difficulties never existed for Dr. Inglis, and were barely so much as thought of in connection with any cause she might have at heart. This, with her clear head and strong common sense, made her a real driving power, and any scheme which had her interest always owed much to her ability to push things through."

In the following chapters the principal events in her life during these twenty years—1894 to 1914—will be dealt with in detail, before we arrive at the story of the last three years and of the "Going Forth."

FOOTNOTES:

[8] From contributions to *Dr. Elsie Inglis*, by Lady Frances Balfour.
[9] *Dr. Elsie Inglis*, by Lady Frances Balfour.

Chapter IV

HER MEDICAL CAREER

1894-1914

During the years from 1894 to 1914 the main stream in Elsie Inglis's life was her medical work. This was her profession, her means of livelihood; it was also the source from which she drew conclusions in various directions, which influenced her conduct in after-years, and it supplied the foundation and the scaffolding for the structure of her achievements at home and abroad.

The pursuit of her profession for twenty years in Edinburgh brought to her many experiences which roused new and wide interests, and which left their impress on her mind.

One who was a fellow-student writes of her classmate: "She impressed one immediately with her mental and physical sturdiness. She had an extremely pleasant face, with a finely moulded forehead, soft, kind, fearless, blue eyes, and a smile, when it came, like sunshine; with this her mouth and chin were firm and determined."

She was a student of the School of Medicine for Women in Edinburgh of which Dr. Jex-Blake was Dean—a fine woman of strong character, to whom, and to a small group of fellow-workers in England, women owe the opening of the door of the medical profession. As Dean, however, she may have erred in attempting an undue control over the students. To Elsie Inglis and some of her fellow-students this seemed to prejudice their liberty, and to frustrate an aim she always had in view, the recognition by the public of an equal footing on all grounds with men students. The difficulties became so great that Elsie Inglis at length left the Edinburgh school and continued her education at Glasgow, where at St. Margaret's College classes in medicine had recently been opened. A fellow-student writes: "Never very keenly interested in the purely scientific side of the curriculum, she had a masterly grasp of what was practical." She took her qualifying medical diploma in 1902.

After her return to Edinburgh she started a scheme and brought it to fruition with that fearlessness and ability which at a later period came to be expected from her, both by her friends and by the public. With the help of sympathetic lecturers and friends of The Women's Movement, she succeeded in establishing a second School of Medicine for Women in Edinburgh, with its headquarters at Minto House, a building which had been associated with the study of medicine since the days of Syme. It proved a successful venture. After the close of Dr. Jex-Blake's school a few years later, it was the only school for women students in Edinburgh, and continued to be so till the University opened its doors to them.

It was mainly due to Dr. Inglis's exertions that The Hospice was opened in the High Street of Edinburgh as a nursing home and maternity centre staffed by medical women. An account of it and of Dr. Inglis's work in connection with it is given in a later chapter.

She was appointed Joint-Surgeon to the Edinburgh Bruntsfield Hospital and Dispensary for Women and Children, also staffed by women and one of the fruits of Dr. Jex-Blake's exertions. Here, again, Elsie Inglis's courage and energy made themselves felt. She desired a larger field for the usefulness of the institution, and proposed to enlarge the hospital to such an extent that its accommodation for patients should be doubled. A colleague writes: "Once again the number must be doubled, always with the same idea in view—*i.e.*, to insure the possibilities for gaining experience for women doctors. Once again the committee was carried along on a wave of unprecedented effort to raise money. An eager band of volunteers was organized, among them some of her own students. Bazaars and entertainments were arranged, special appeals were issued, and the necessary money was found, and the alterations carried out. It was never part of Dr. Inglis's policy to wait till the money came in. She always played a bold game, and took risks which left the average person aghast, and in the end she invariably justified her action by accomplishing the task which she set herself, and, at times it must be owned, which she set an all too unwilling committee! But for that breezy and invincible faith and optimism the Scottish Women's Hospitals would never have taken shape in 1914."

23

Dr. Inglis's plea for the Units of the Scottish Women's Hospital was always that they might be sent "where the need was greatest." In these years of work before the war the same motive, to supply help where it was most needed, seems to have guided her private practice, for we read: "Dr. Inglis was perhaps seen at her best in her dispensary work, for she was truly the friend and the champion of the working woman, and especially of the mother in poor circumstances and struggling to bring up a large family. Morrison Street Dispensary and St. Anne's Dispensary were the centre of this work, and for years to come mothers will be found in this district who will relate how Dr. Inglis put at their service the best of her professional skill and, more than that, gave them unstintedly of her sympathy and understanding."

Dr. Wallace Williamson, of St. Giles's Cathedral, writing of her after her death, is conscious also of this impulse always manifesting itself in her to work where difficulties abounded. He points out: "Of her strictly professional career it may be truly said that her real attraction had been to work among the suffering poor.... She was seen at her best in hospice and dispensary, and in homes where poverty added keenness to pain. There she gave herself without reserve. Questions of professional rivalry or status of women slipped away in her large sympathy and helpfulness. Like a truly 'good physician,' she gave them from her own courage an uplift of spirit even more valuable than physical cure. She understood them and was their friend. To her they were not merely patients, but fellow-women. It was one of her great rewards that the poor folk to whom she gave of her best rose to her faith in them, whatever their privations or temptations. Her relations with them were remote from mere routine, and so distinctively human and real that her name is everywhere spoken with the note of personal loss. Had not the wider call come, this side of her work awaited the fulfilment of ever nobler dreams."

She was loved and appreciated as a doctor not only by her poorer patients, but by those whom she attended in all ranks of society.

Of her work as an operator and lecturer two of her colleagues say:

"It was a pleasure to see Dr. Inglis in the operating-theatre. She was quiet, calm, and collected, and never at a loss, skilful in her manipulations, and able to cope with any emergency."

"As a lecturer she proved herself clear and concise, and the level of her lectures never fell below that of the best established standards. Students were often heard to say that they owed to her a clear and a practical grasp of a subject which is inevitably one of the most important for women doctors."

Should it be asked what was the secret of her success in her work, the answer would not be difficult to find. A clear brain she had, but she had more. She had vision, for her life was based on a profound trust in God, and her vision was that of a follower of Christ, the vision of the kingdom of heaven upon earth. This was the true source of that remarkable optimism which carried her over difficulties deemed by others insurmountable. Once started in pursuit of an object, she was most reluctant to abandon it, and her gaze was so keenly fixed on the end in view that it must be admitted she was found by some to be "ruthless" in the way in which she pushed on one side any who seemed to her to be delaying or obstructing the fulfilment of her project. There was, however, never any selfish motive prompting her; the end was always a noble one, for she had an unselfish, generous nature. An intimate friend, well qualified to judge, herself at first prejudiced against her, writes:

"In everything she did that was always to me her most outstanding characteristic, her self-effacing and abounding generosity. Indeed, it was so characteristic of her that it was often misunderstood and her action was imputed to a desire for self-advertisement. A fellow-doctor told me that when she was working in one of the Edinburgh laboratories she heard men discussing something Dr. Inglis had undertaken, and, evidently finding her action quite incomprehensible, they concluded it was dictated by personal ambition. My friend turned on them in the most emphatic way: 'You were never more mistaken. The thought of self or self-interest never even entered Elsie Inglis's mind in anything she did or said.'" Again, another writes: "One recalls her generous appreciation of any good work done by other women, especially by younger women. Any attempt to strike out in a new line, any attempt to fill a post not previously occupied by a woman, received her unstinted admiration and warm support."

It was her delight to show hospitality to her friends, many of whom, especially women doctors and friends made in the Suffrage movement, stayed with her at her house in Walker Street, Edinburgh. But her hospitality did not end there. One doctor, whom we have already quoted, on arrival on a visit, found that only the day before Dr. Inglis had said good-bye to a party of guests, a woman with five children, a patient badly in need of rest, who had the misfortune to have an unhappy home, and was without any relatives to help her. Dr. Inglis's relations with her poor patients have been already referred to. Not only did she give them all she could in the way of professional attention and skill, but her generosity to them was unbounded. "I had a patient," writes a doctor, "very ill with pulmonary tuberculosis. She was to go to a sanatorium, and her widowed mother was quite unable to provide the rather ample outfit demanded. Dr. Inglis gave me everything for her, down to umbrella and goloshes."

Naturally her devotion was returned, though in one case which is recorded Dr. Inglis's care met with resentment at first. A woman who was expecting a baby—her ninth—applied at a dispensary where Dr. Inglis happened to be in charge. Her advice was distasteful to the patient, who tried another dispensary, only to meet again with the same advice, again from a woman member of the profession. A third dispensary brought her the same fortune! Eventually, when the need for professional skill came, she was attended by the two latter doctors she had seen, for the case proved to be a difficult one. Requiring the aid of greater experience—for they were juniors—they sent for Dr. Inglis, with whose help the lives of mother and child were saved. Thus the patient was attended in the end by all the three women physicians whose advice she had scorned. The child was the first boy in the large family, and the mother's gratitude and delight after her recovery knew no bounds. It found, however, Scotch expression, shall we say? in her tribute, "Weel, I've had the hale three o' ye efter a', and ye canna say I hae'na likit ye—*at the hinder en' at ony rate*!" "That woman kept us busy with patients for many a day," writes one of the three. The bulky mother-in-law of one patient expressed her admiration of the doctor and her lack of faith in the justice of things by saying: "It's no fair Dr. Inglis is a woman; if she'd been a man, she'd ha' been a millionaire!" The doctor in whose memory these incidents live says of her friend: "No item was too trivial, no trouble too great to take, if she could help a human being, or if she could push forward or help a younger doctor."

If Elsie Inglis's intrepidity, determination, and invincible optimism were well known to the public, the circle of her friends was warmed by the truly loving heart with which they came in contact.

The following incident may show in some degree what a tender heart it was. A friend whose brother died, after an operation, in a nursing home in Edinburgh was staying at Dr. Inglis's house when the death occurred. The body had to be taken to the Highland home in the North. The sister writes: "My younger brother called for me in the early morning, as we had to leave by the 3 a.m. train to accompany the body to Inverness. When Dr. Inglis had said good-bye to us and we drove away in the cab, my brother—he is just an ordinary keen business man—turned to me with his eyes filled with tears, and said: 'I should have liked to kiss her like my mother.' (We had never known our mother.)"

In the fourteenth century, in that wonderful and most lovable woman, Catherine of Siena, we find the same union of strength and tenderness which was so noticeable in Dr. Inglis. In the *Life* of St. Catherine it is said: "Everybody loves Catherine Benincasa because she was always and everywhere a woman in every fibre of her being. By nature and temperament she was fitted to be what she succeeded in remaining to the end—a strong, noble woman, whose greatest strength lay in her tenderness, and whose nobility sprung from her tender femininity."

In her political sagacity, her optimism, and cheerfulness also, she reminds us of Elsie Inglis. During St. Catherine's Mission to Tuscany the following story is told of her by her biographer: "The other case" (of healing) "was that of Messer Matteo, her friend, the Rector of Misericordia, who had been one of the most active of the heretic priests in Siena. To this good man, lying *in extremis* after terrible agony, Catherine entered, crying cheerfully: 'Rise up, rise up, Ser Matteo! This is not the time to be taking your ease in bed!' Immediately the disease left him, and he, who could so ill be spared at such a time, arose whole and sound to minister to others."[10]

We smile as we read of Catherine's "cheerful" entrance into this sick-chamber, and those who knew Dr. Inglis can recall many such a breezy entrance into the depressing atmosphere of some of her patients' sickrooms.

FOOTNOTE:

[10] *Catherine of Siena*, by C. M. Antony.

Chapter V

THE SOLVED PROBLEMS

"It is the solution worked out in the life, not merely in words, that brings home to other lives the fact that the problem is not insoluble."

It may be truly said that special types of problems come before the unmarried woman for solution—problems as to her connection with society and with the race, which confront her as they do not others. Though few signs of a mental struggle were visible on the surface, there is no doubt that Elsie Inglis met these problems and settled them in the silence of her heart. It is a fact of much interest in connection with the subject of this memoir that amongst the papers found after she had died is the MS. of a novel written by herself, entitled *The Story of a Modern Woman*, and one turns the pages with eager interest to see if they furnish a key to the path along which she travelled in solving her problems. The expectation is realized, and in reading the pages of the novel we find the secret of the assurance and happy courage which characterized her. Whether she intended it or not, many parts of the book are without doubt autobiographical. In this chapter we propose to give some extracts from the novel which we consider justify the belief that the authoress is describing her own experiences.

The first extract refers to her "discovery" that she was almost entirely without fear. The heroine is Hildeguard Forrest, a woman of thirty-seven, a High School teacher. During a boating accident, which might have resulted fatally, the fact reveals itself to Hildeguard that she does not know what fear is. The story of the accident closes with these words:

"Self-revelation is not usually a pleasant process. Not often do we find ourselves better than we expected. Usually the sudden flash that shows us ourselves makes us blush with shame at the sight we see. But very rarely, and for the most part for the people who are not self-conscious, the flash may, in a moment, reveal unknown powers or unsuspected strength.

"And Hildeguard, sitting back in the boat, suddenly realized she wasn't a coward. She looked back in surprise over her life, and remembered that the terror which as a child would seize her in a sudden emergency was the fear of being parted from her mother, not any personal fear for herself, or her own safety.

"Such a pleasurable glow swept over her as she sat there in the rocking boat. 'Why, no,' she thought; 'I wasn't frightened.'"

A similar accident befell Elsie Inglis when a young woman. Whether the absence of fear disclosed itself to her then or not cannot be said, but she is known to have said to a friend after her return from Serbia: "It was a great day in my life when I discovered that I did not know what fear was."

Benjamin Kidd in *The Science of Power* gives (unintentionally) an indication where to look for the secret of the childless woman's feeling of loneliness—*she has no link with the future*. He affirms that woman because of her very nature has her roots in the future. "To women," he says, "the race is always more than the individual; the future greater than the present."

As we follow Hildeguard through the pages of the novel, she is shown to us as faced with the problem of becoming "a lonely woman," the problem that meets the unmarried and the childless woman. And the claims and the meaning of religion are confronting her too. The story traces the workings of Hildeguard's mind and the events of her life for a year.

Christmas Day in the novel finds Hildeguard a lonely and dissatisfied woman with no "sure anchor." She has had a happy childhood, with many relations and friends around her. One by one these are taken from her—some are dead, others are married—and she sees herself, at the age of thirty-seven, a forlorn figure with no great interest in the future, and her thoughts dwelling mostly on the joyous past. Two or three of Hildeguard's friends are conversing together in her rooms. None of them has had a happy day. Each in her own way is feeling the depression of the lonely woman. Frances, a little Quaker lady, enters the room, as someone remarks on the sadness of Christmas-time.

"'Yes,' at last said the Quaker lady; 'I heard what you said as I came in, dear. Christmas is a hard time with all its memories. *I think I have found out what we lonely women want. It is a future.* Our thoughts are always turning to the past. There is not anything to link us on to the next generation. You see other women with their families—it is the future to which they look. However good the past has been, they expect more to come, for their sons and their daughters. Their life goes on in other lives.' Hildeguard clasped her hands round her knees and stared into the fire."

"Their life goes on in other lives"—the thought finds a home in Hildeguard's mind. When, soon after, the little Quakeress dies, Hildeguard, looking at the quiet face, says to herself: "*Dear little woman! So you have got your future.*" But in her own case she does not wait for death to bring it to her; she faces her problems, and, refusing to be swamped by them, makes the currents carry her bark along to the free, open sea. She flings herself whole-heartedly into causes whose hopes rest in the future. She draws around her children, who need her love and care, and makes them her hostages for the future. In all this we see Elsie Inglis describing a stage in her own life.

But before the story brings us round again to Christmas, something else has helped to change the outlook for Hildeguard; she has found herself in relation to God. Her religion is no merely inherited thing—not hers at second-hand, this "link with God." It is a real thing to her, found for herself, made part of herself, and so her sure foundation. It has come to her in a flash, a never-to-be-forgotten illumination of the words: "*The Power of an Endless Life.*" She faces life now glad and free.

In her "den" on that Christmas Eve she is described thus to us by Elsie Inglis:

"Ann had put holly berries over the pictures, and the mantelpiece, too, was covered with it. Between the masses of green and the red berries stood the solid, old-fashioned, gilt frames of long ago, the photographs in them becoming yellow with age. Hildeguard turned to them from the portraits on the walls. She stood, her hands resting on the edge of the mantelpiece. Then suddenly it came to her that her whole attitude towards life and death had altered. For long these old photographs had stood to her as symbols of a past glowing with happiness. Though the pain still lingered even after time had dulled the edge, yet the old pictures typified all that was best in life, and the dim mist of the years rose up between the good days and her.

"But now, as she looked, her thoughts did not turn to the past. In some unexplained way the loves of long ago seemed to be entwined with a future so wonderful and so enticing that her heart bounded as she thought of it.

31

"'Grow old along with me; The best is yet to be.'

"Only last Christmas those words would have meant nothing to her. Then her bark seemed to be stranded among shallows. She felt that she was an old woman, and 'second bests' her lot in the coming years. There could never be any life equal to the old life, in the back-water into which she had drifted.

"But to-day how different the outlook! Her ship was flying over a sunlit sea, the good wind bulging out the canvas. She felt the thrill of excitement and adventure in her veins as she stood at the helm and gazed across the dancing water. It seemed to her as if she had been asleep and the "Celestial Surgeon" had come and 'stabbed her spirit broad awake.' Joy had done its work, and sorrow; responsibility had come with its stimulating spur, and the ardent delight of battle in a great crusade. New powers she had discovered in herself, new possibilities in the world around her. She was ready for her 'adventure brave and new.' Rabbi Ben Ezra had waited for death to open the gate to it, but to Hildeguard it seemed that she was in the midst of it now, that 'adventure brave and new' in which death itself was also an adventure.

"'The Power of an Endless Life'—the words seemed to hover around her, just eluding her grasp, just beyond her comprehension, yet something of their significance she seemed to catch. She remembered the flash of intuition as she stood beside Frances' newly-made grave, but she realized, her eyes on the old pictures, that it would take æons to understand all it meant, to exhaust all the wonder of the idea. She could only bring to it her undeveloped powers of thought and of imagination, but she knew that stretching away, hid in an inexpressible light, lay depths undreamt of. To her nineteenth-century intellect life could only mean evolution—life ever taking to itself new forms, developing itself in new ways. At the bed-rock of all her thought lay the consciousness of 'the Power not ourselves, which makes for Righteousness.'

"No mystic she, to whom an ineffable union with the Highest was the goal of all. Never even distantly did she reach to that idea. Rather she was one of God's simple-hearted soldiers, who took her orders and stood to her post. The words thrilled her, not with the prospect of rest, but with the excitement of advance, 'an Endless Life' with ever new possibilities of growth and of achievement, ever greater battles to be fought for the right, and always new hopes of happiness. Doubtingly and hesitatingly she committed herself to the thought, conscious that it had been forming slowly and unregarded in the strenuous months that lay behind her, through the long years, ever since the first seemingly hopeless 'good-bye' had wrung her heart. She began dimly to feel the 'power' of the idea, the life of which she was the holder, only 'part of a greater whole.' Earth itself only a step in a great progression. Ever upward, ever onward, marching towards some 'Divine far-off event, to which the whole creation moves.'"

If another pen than Elsie Inglis's had drawn the picture we should have said it was one of herself. Surely she was able to weave around her heroine, from the depth of her own inner experiences of solved problems, the mantle of joy and freedom with which she herself was clothed.

The causes to which Elsie Inglis became a tower of strength; the "nation she twice saved from despair"; the many children, not only those in her own connection, on whom she lavished love and care, are the witnesses to-day of the completeness and the splendour of her power to mould each adverse circumstance in her life and make it yield a great advantage.

Chapter VI

"HER CHILDREN"

"Wonderful courage," "intrepidity of action," "strength of purpose," "no weakening pity"—these are terms that are often used in describing Elsie Inglis. But there is another side to her character, not so well known, from its very nature bound to be less known, which it is the purpose of this chapter to discover.

Elsie Inglis was a very loving woman, and she was a child-lover. From every source that touched her life, and, touching it, brought her into contact with child-life, she, by her interest in children, drew to herself this healing link with the future. The children of her poorer patients knew well the place they held in her heart. "They would watch from the windows, on her dispensary days, for her, and she would wave to them across the street. She would often stop them in the street, and ask after their mother, and even after she had been to Serbia and had returned to Edinburgh she remembered them and their home affairs."[11]

The daily letters to her father, written from Glasgow and London and Dublin, are full of stories about the children of her patients. Who but a genuine child-lover could have found time to write to a little niece, under twelve, letters from Serbia and Russia—one in August, 1915, during "The Long, Peaceful Summer," and the other in an ambulance train near Odessa?

Her book, *The Story of a Modern Woman*, contains many descriptions which reveal a mind to whom the ways of children are of deep interest. We draw once more from the pages of the novel, as in no other way can we show so well the mother-heart that was hers.

One of Hildeguard's friends, dying in India, leaves three small children, whom she commends to her pity. Hildeguard's heart responds at once, and the orphans find their home with her. Her first meeting with the frightened children and their black nurse is described in detail:

"'Just let's wait a minute or two,' said Hildeguard. 'Let them get used to me. Well, Baby,' she said, turning to the ayah, and holding out her arms.

"With a great leap and a gurgle Baby precipitated himself towards her, his strong little hands clutching uncertainly at the brooch at her throat. Then the buttons distracted him, and then, after a serious look at her face, his eyes suddenly caught sight of the hat above it, and the irresistible gleam of some ornament on it. With wildly working hands he pulled himself to his feet, and, with one fat little hand on her face, grabbed at the shining jet.

"Hildeguard, laughing, and submitting herself half resistingly to the onslaught, felt her hat dragged sideways by the uncertain little hand.

"She held the little one close to her, still laughing, kissing the firm little arms and hands, and talking baby nonsense as if it had been her mother-tongue for years.

"The brooch again caught Baby's eye, and he made another determined raid on it. He seized it and pricked his finger. Down went the corners of his mouth.

"'There now,' said Hildeguard, 'I knew you'd do that, you duckie boy,' kissing the pricked hand over and over again. 'And good little sonnie is not to cry. A watch is much safer than a brooch: now let's see if we can get at it,' feeling in her belt.

"The watch was grabbed at and went straight to his mouth.

"'Does your watch blow open?' asked Rex.

"'Come and see,' said Hildeguard.

"Rex came without a moment's hesitation. Eileen was forgotten in the interest of a new investigation. The watch did blow open. How exceedingly exciting! He leaned both arms on Hildeguard's knee while he defended the watch from Baby's greedy attacks. Then he suddenly remembered something of more importance.

"'I've got a watch too.' He wriggled wildly with excitement, and pulled out a Waterbury.

"'Well, you are a lucky boy!' said Hildeguard.

"Eileen had come forward too, but Hildeguard waited for her to speak before noticing the advance. Rex was standing near to her, pointing out the beauties of the watch, the hands, etc.

"'And—and—bigger like that'—stretching his arms wide—'bigger like that than your watch.'

"'Your watch,' said Eileen, 'is little and tiny, like Mummy's watch. But

Mummy's watch pins on here,' dabbing at Hildeguard's blouse. Then suddenly she raised swimming eyes to Hildeguard's: 'I do want Mummy,' she said.

"'Darling,' cried Hildeguard, catching Baby with her right arm, so as to free the other to draw Eileen to her—'Darling, so we all do.'"

It is a simple account of the little ways of shy children. Many a mother could have written it equally well.

But the interest of Elsie Inglis's descriptions of children lies in the fact that they come from the pen of a woman of action, a woman of iron nerve, and they give us the other side of her character.

And then—she was a woman whom no child called mother! But thank God the instinct is not one that can be dammed up or lost, and in these writings we get a glimpse of that motherhood which was hers, and which her life showed to be deep enough and wide enough to sweep under its wing the human souls, men, women, and children, who, passing near it, and being in need, cried out for help, and never cried in vain. To quote a fellow-woman:

"The emotions which are the strongest force in a woman must not live in the past; they must not be used introspectively, nor for personal pleasure and gratification. Used thus, they destroy the woman and weaken the race. But *flung forward*, flung into interests outside of the woman herself, and thus transmuted into power, they become to her her salvation, and to the race a constructive element."

FOOTNOTE:

[11] *Dr. Elsie Inglis*, by Lady Frances Balfour.

36

Chapter VII

THE HOSPICE

During her medical career Dr. Inglis never lost sight of one aim, equal opportunity for the woman with the man in all branches of education and practical training and responsibility. She recognized that young women doctors in Edinburgh suffered under a serious disadvantage in being ineligible for the post of resident medical officer in the Royal Infirmary and the chief maternity hospital. "But," writes a friend, "it was characteristic of her and her inherent inability to visualize obstacles except as incentive to greater effort that she set herself to remedy this disadvantage instead of accepting it as an insurmountable difficulty. *Women doctors must found a maternity hospital of their own.* That was her first decision. A committee was formed, and the public responded generously to an appeal for funds." Through the kindness of Dr. Hugh Barbour, a house in George Square was put at the committee's disposal. But Dr. Inglis felt that it must be near the homes of the poor women who needed its shelter, and after four years a site was chosen in the historic High Street. Three stories in a huge "tenement," reached by a narrow winding stair, were adapted, and The Hospice opened its doors.

It was opened in 1901 as a hospital for women, with a dispensary and out-patient department, admitting cases of accident and general illness as well as maternity patients. After nine years, it was decided to draft the general cases from the district to the Edinburgh Hospital for Women and Children, and The Hospice devoted all its beds to maternity cases.

THE HOSPICE, HIGH STREET, EDINBURGH

Photo by D. Scott

THE HOSPICE, HIGH STREET, EDINBURGH

As soon as the admission book showed a steady intake of patients, Dr. Inglis applied for and secured recognition as a lecturer for the Central Midwifery Board, in order to be in a position to admit resident pupils (nurses and students) to The Hospice for practical instruction in midwifery. She at the same time applied to the University of Edinburgh for recognition as an extramural lecturer on gynæcology. Recognition was granted, and for some years she lectured, using The Hospice or the Edinburgh Hospital for Women and Children at Bruntsfield Place for her practical instruction.

A woman doctor writes: "In thus starting a maternity hospital in the heart of this poor district she showed the understanding born of her long experience in the High Street and her great sympathy for all women in their hour of need. Single-handed she developed a maternity indoor and district service, training her nurses herself in anticipation of the extension of the Midwives Act to Scotland. Never too tired to turn out at night as well as by day, cheerfully taking on the necessary lecturing, she always worked to lay such a foundation that a properly equipped maternity hospital would be the natural outcome."

Though hampered by lack of money and suitable assistance, she was never daunted, and in a characteristic way insisted that all necessary medical requirements should be met, whatever the expense. She worked at The Hospice with devotion. Though cherishing always her aim of an institution which, while serving the poor, should provide a training for women doctors, she threw herself heart and soul into the work because she loved it for its own sake, and she loved her poor patients.

In 1913 Dr. Inglis went to America, and her letters were full of her plans for further development on her return. At Muskegon, Michigan, she found a small memorial hospital, of which she wrote enthusiastically as the exact thing she wanted for midwifery in Edinburgh.

On returning from America, for a time she was far from well, and one of her colleagues, in September, 1913, urged her to forgo her hard work at The Hospice, begging her to take things more easily.

Her reply, in a moment of curious concentration and earnestness, was characteristic: "Give me one more year; I know there is a future there, and someone will be found to take it on." A year later, when it seemed inevitable that it must come to an end with her departure for Serbia, those interested in

38

The Hospice passed through deep waters in saving it, but the unanswerable argument against closing its doors was always that big circle of patients, often pleading her name, flocking up its stair, certain of help.

"Three things foreseen by Dr. Inglis have happened since her departure:

"1. The extension of the Midwives Act to Scotland, establishing recognized training centres for midwifery nursing.

"2. The extension of Notification of Births Act, making State co-operation in maternity service possible.

"3. The admission of women medical students to the University, making an opportunity for midwifery training in Edinburgh of immediate and paramount importance.

"The relation of The Hospice to these three events is as follows:

"1. It is now fourth on the list of recognized training centres in Scotland, following the three large maternity hospitals.

"2. It is incorporated in the Maternity and Child Welfare scheme of Edinburgh, which assists in out-patient work, though not in the provision of beds.

"3. It has full scope under the Ordinances of the Scottish Universities to train women medical students in Clinical Midwifery if it had a sufficient number of beds.

"The Hospice has the distinction of being the only maternity training centre run by women in Scotland. From this point of view it is of great value to women students, affording them opportunities of study denied to them in other maternity hospitals.

"To those of her friends who knew her Edinburgh life intimately, Elsie Inglis's love of The Hospice was the love of a mother for her child. She was never too tired or too busy to respond to any demand its patients made upon her time and energy, always ready to go anywhere in crowded close, or remote tenement, if it was to see a mother who had once been an in-patient there or a baby born within its walls. True, Dr. Inglis saw The Hospice with romantic eyes, with that vision of future perfection which is the seal of pure romance in motherhood. Because of this she cheerfully accepted those cramped and inconvenient flats, reached by the narrow common stair which vanishes past The Hospice door in a corkscrew flight to regions under the roof. Inconvenience and straitened quarters were as nothing, for was not her Nursing Home exactly where she wished it, with the ebb and flow of the High Street at its feet? Dr. Inglis always rejoiced greatly in the High Street, in the charm of the precincts of St. Giles, that ineffable Heart of Midlothian, serenely catholic, brooding upon the motley life that has surged for centuries about its doors. Here, where she loved to be, The Hospice is finding a new home, an adequate building, modern equipment, and endowed beds, and it will stand a living memorial, communicating to all who pass in and out of its doors, to women in need, to women strong to help, the inspiration of Dr. Elsie Inglis's ideal of service."

Chapter VIII

.

THE SUFFRAGE CAMPAIGN

The question of Woman's Suffrage had always interested Dr. Inglis, for the justice of the claim had from the first appealed to her. But it was not until after 1900 that the Women's Movement took possession of her. From that time onward, till the Scottish Women's Hospitals claimed her in the war, the cause of Woman's Suffrage demanded and was granted a place in her life beside that occupied by her profession. Indeed, the very practice of her profession added fuel to the flame that the longing for the Suffrage had kindled in her heart. A doctor sees much of the intimate life of her patients, and as Dr. Inglis went from patient to patient, conditions amongst both the poor and the rich—intolerable conditions—would raise haunting thoughts that followed her about in her work, and questions again and again start up to which only the Suffrage could give the answer. The Suffrage flame with her, as with many other women and men, was really one which religion tended; it was religious conviction which mastered her and made her eager and dauntless in the fight. She always worked from the constitutional point of view, and was an admirer and follower of Mrs. Fawcett throughout the campaign.

"As she threw herself into this new interest she found a gale of fresh air blowing through her life. It was almost as if she had awakened on a new morning. The sunshine flooded every nook and corner of her dwelling, and even old things looked different in the new light. Not the least of these impressions was due to the new friendships; women whose life-work was farthest from her own, whose point of view was diametrically opposite to hers, suddenly drew up beside her in the march as comrades. She felt as if she had got a wider outlook over the world, as if in her upward climb she had reached a spur on the hillside, and a new view of the landscape spread itself at her feet.

"As she had once said, fate had placed her in the van of a great movement, but she herself clung to old forms and old ways—a new thing she

41

instinctively avoided. It took her long to adjust herself to a new point of view. But here, in this absorbing interest, she forgot everything but the object. Her eyes had suddenly been opened to what it meant to be a citizen of Britain, and in the overpowering sense of responsibility that came with the revelation her timorous clinging to old ways had slackened.

"Not the least part of the interest of the new life was the feeling of being at the centre of things. People whose names had been household words since babyhood became living entities. She not only saw the men and women who were moulding our generation: she met them at tea, she talked intimately with them at dinners, and she actually argued with them at Council meetings."

Thus Elsie Inglis describes in her writings her heroine Hildeguard's entrance into "the great crusade." The description may be taken as true of her own feelings when caught by the ideal of the movement.

The following words which she puts into the mouth of a Suffrage speaker are evidently her own reflections on the subject of the Suffrage:

"'I don't think for a moment that the millennium will come in with the vote,' she smiled, after a little pause. 'But our faces, the faces of the human race, have always been set towards the millennium, haven't they? And this will be one great step towards it. It is always difficult to make a move forward, for it implies criticism of the past, and of the good men and true who have brought the people up to that especial point. However gently the change is made, that element must be there, for there is always a sense of struggle in changing from the old to the new. I do not think we are nearly careful enough to make it quite clear that we do not hold that we women *alone* could have done a bit better—that we are proud of the great work our men have done. We speak only of the mistakes, not of the great achievements; only I do think the mistakes need not have been there if we had worked at it together!'

"The salvation of the world was wrapped up in the gospel she preached. Many of the audience were caught in the swirl as she spoke. Love and amity, the common cause of healthier homes and happier people and a stronger Empire, the righting of all wrongs, and the strengthening of all right—all this was wrapped up in the vote."

In the early years of this century Suffrage societies were scattered all over Scotland, and it began to be felt that much of their work was lost from want of co-operation; it was therefore decided in 1906 that all the societies should form a federation, to be called the Scottish Federation of Women's Suffrage Societies.

During the preliminary work Mrs. James T. Hunter acted as Hon. Secretary, but after the headquarters were established in Edinburgh Dr. Inglis was asked and consented to be Hon. Secretary, with Miss Lamont as Organizing Secretary. There is no doubt that after its formation the success of the Federation was largely due to Dr. Inglis's power of leadership.

She cheered the faithful—if sometimes despondent—suffragists in widely scattered centres; she despised the difficulties of travel in the north, and over moor, mountain, and sea she went, till she had planted the Suffrage flag in far-off Shetland. In her many journeys all over Scotland, speaking for the Suffrage cause, Dr. Inglis herself penetrated to the islands of Orkney and Shetland. A very flourishing Society existed in the Orkneys.

The following letter from Dr. Inglis to the Honorary Secretary there is characteristic, and will recall her vividly to those who knew her. The arrival for the meeting by the last train; the early start back next morning; the endeavour to see her friend's daughter, who she remembers is in Dollar; the light-heartedness over "disasters in the House" (evidently the setback to some Suffrage Bill in the House of Commons)—these are all like Elsie Inglis. So, too, are her praise of the Federation secretaries, her eager looking forward to the procession, and the request for the "beautiful banner"!

1913.

"Dear Mrs. Cursiter,

"Yes, I had remembered your daughter is at Dollar, and I shall certainly look out for her at the meeting. Unfortunately, I never have time to stay in a place, at one of these meetings, and see people. It would often be so pleasant. This time I arrive in Dollar at 6 p.m. and leave about 8 the next morning. I have to leave by these early trains for my work.

"It was delightful getting your offer of an organizer's salary for some work in Orkney. Our secretaries have been most extraordinarily unconcerned over disasters in the House! Not one of you has suggested depression, and most of you have promptly proposed new work! That is the sort of spirit that wins.

"I shall let you know definitely about an organizer soon.

"At the Executive on Saturday it was decided to have a procession in Edinburgh during the Assembly week. We shall want you and your beautiful banner! You'll get full particulars soon.

"Yours very sincerely,

"Elsie Maud Inglis."

One of the Federation organizers who worked under Dr. Inglis for years gives us some indication of her qualities as a leader:

"Though it was not unknown that Dr. Inglis had an extraordinary influence over young people, it was amazing to find how many letters were received after her death from young women in various parts of the kingdom, who wrote to express what they owed to her sympathy and encouragement.

"To be a leader one must be able not only to inspire confidence in the leader, but to give to those who follow confidence in themselves, and this, I think, was one of Dr. Inglis's most outstanding qualities. She would select one of her workers, and after unfolding her plans to her, would quietly say, 'Now, my dear, I want you to undertake that piece of work for me.' As often as not the novice's breath was completely taken away; she would demur, and remark that she was afraid she was not quite the right person to be entrusted with that special piece of work. Then the Chief would give her one of those winning smiles which none could resist, and tell her she was quite confident she would not fail. The desired result was usually attained, and the young worker gained more confidence in herself. If, on the other hand, the worker failed to complete her task satisfactorily, Dr. Inglis would discuss the matter with her. She might condemn, but never unjustly, and would then arrange another opportunity for the worker in a different department of the work.

"From those with whom she worked daily she expected great things. She was herself an unceasing worker, well-nigh indefatigable. It was no easy matter to work under 'the Chief's' direction; the possibility of failure never entered into her calculations."

One of the finest speakers in the Suffrage cause, who with her husband worked hard in the campaign, frequently stayed with Dr. Inglis. She writes thus of her:

"With me it is always most difficult to speak about the things upon which I feel the most deeply. Elsie Inglis is a case in point. She was dearer to me than she ever knew and than I can make you believe. She is one of the most precious memories I possess, the mere thought of her and her tireless devotion to her fellows being the strongest inspiration to effort and achievement.

"She was the Edinburgh hostess for most of the Woman Suffrage propagandists, and we all have the same story to tell. Doubtless you have already had it from others. Every comfort she denied herself she scrupulously provided for her guests, whom she treated as though they were more tired than herself. Usually she was at her medical work till within a few minutes of the evening meal, would rush home and eat it with us, take us to the meeting afterwards, frequently take a part in it, and bring her guests home to the rest she was not always permitted to take herself. And through it all there was no variation in her wonderful manner—all brightness, affection, and warm energy.

"The last time I saw her was in the Waverley station. She was returning shortly to her work abroad, while I was on my way to address a public meeting in Dundee on the need for attempting to negotiate peace. It was the time when everybody who dared to breathe the word 'peace,' much more those who tried to stop the slaughter of men, were denounced as traitors and pro-Germans. It was the time when one's nearest and dearest failed to understand. But *she* understood. And she broke into a busy morning's work to come down to the train to shake my hand. What we said was very little; but the look and the hand-clasp were sufficient. We knew ourselves to be serving the same God of Love and Mercy, and that knowledge made the bonds between us indissoluble. I never saw nor had word with her again.

"It is easy to say, what is true, that the world's women owe to Dr. Elsie Inglis a debt of gratitude they can never repay. But I am convinced in my own soul that the reward she would have chosen, if compelled to make the choice, would have been that all who feel that her work was of worth should join hands in an effort to rid the world of those evils which make men and women hate and kill one another."

Dr. Inglis did not see with the pacifists of the last five years. But in this tribute to her is shown her open-mindedness and tolerance of another's views, even on this cleaving difference of opinion.

A woman of great distinction—and not only in the Suffrage movement—says:

"When I was working for the Suffrage movement in the years before the war, one of the most impressive personalities that I came into touch with was that of Dr. Elsie Inglis. She was then the leading spirit in our movement in Edinburgh, and when I went to speak there, or in the neighbourhood, she always used to put me up. I have never met anyone who seemed to me more absolutely single-minded and single-hearted in her devotion to a cause which appealed to her. She was eminently a feminist, and to her feminism she subordinated everything else. No consideration for her health, for her position, for her practice, ever stood in the way of any call that came to her. She was untiring, and that at a time when our cause was not popular everywhere, and when her position as a medical woman might easily have been affected by its unpopularity.

"I remember one night especially, when we were going out in a motor-car to some rather remote place, in very stormy weather. It howled and rained and was pitch dark. Suddenly we ran, or nearly ran, into a great tree which had been blown down across the road. It had brought with it a mass of telegraph wire, and altogether afforded an apparently complete 'barrage.' We were still some six or seven miles from our destination, and were wearing evening frocks and thin shoes. We got out and wrestled with the obstacle, and when at one time it seemed quite hopeless to get the car through, and I suggested that she and I would have to walk, I shall never forget the look of approval that she turned on me. As a matter of fact, I doubt very much whether I really *could* have walked. I am a little lame, and the circumstances made it almost an impossibility. But the determination of Dr. Inglis that somehow we *should* get to our meeting infected me, and, like many others who have followed her since, I felt able to achieve the impossible.

"It is true that Dr. Inglis seemed to me—since, after all, she was human—to have the faults of her qualities. No consideration of herself prevented her complete devotion to her work. I sometimes felt that there was an element of relentlessness in this devotion, which would have allowed her to sacrifice not only other people, but even perhaps considerations which it is not easy to believe ought to be sacrificed. It is extraordinarily difficult to judge how far any end may justify any given means. It is, of course, a shallow judgment which dismisses this dilemma as one easily solved. Rather, I have always felt it exceedingly difficult, at any rate to an intellect that is subtle as well as powerful. I am reminded, in thinking of Dr. Inglis, of the controversy between Kingsley and Newman, from which it appears that Charles Kingsley thought it a very easy matter to tell the truth, and Newman found it a very difficult one. One's judgment of the two will, of course, vary, but I personally have always felt that Newman understood the truth more perfectly than Kingsley; understood, for instance, that it takes two people to tell it (one to speak and one to hear aright), and that this was why he realized its difficulty. So with Dr. Inglis; I do not suppose she ever hesitated when once convinced of the goodness of her cause, but I confess that I have sometimes wished that she could have hesitated.

"It is a graceless task to suggest spots in so excellent a sun, and we feminists who worked with her and loved her can never be glad enough or proud enough that the world now knows the greatness of her quality."

Again, an organizer who worked constantly with Dr. Inglis before the war, and who later raised large sums for the Scottish Women's Hospitals in India and Australia, writes:

"You have asked me for some personal memories of my dear Dr. Elsie Inglis, for some of those little incidents that often reveal a character more vividly than much description and explanation. And to me, at least, it is in some of those little memories that the Dr. Inglis I loved lives most vividly. What I mean is that her splendid public work, in medicine, in Suffrage, in that magnificent triumph of the Scottish Women's Hospitals—they were *her* hospitals—is there for all the world to see and honour. But the things behind all that, the character that conquered, the spirit that aspired, the incredible courage, optimism, indomitability of that individuality, the very self from which the work sprang—all that, it seems to me, had to be gathered in and understood from the tiny incident, the word, the glance.

"There stands out in my mind my first meeting with Dr. Inglis. The scene was dismal and depressing enough. It was an empty shop in an Edinburgh Street turned into a Suffrage committee-room during an election. Outside the rain drizzled; inside the meagre fire smoked; there was a general air of lifelessness over everything. I wondered, ignorant and uninitiated in organizing and election work, when something definite would happen. Giving away sodden handbills in the street did not seem a very vigorous or practical piece of work.

"Suddenly the doors swung open and Dr. Inglis came into that dull place, and with her there came the very feeling of movement, vitality, action. She had come to arrange speakers for the various schoolroom election meetings to be held that night. The list of meeting-places was arranged; then came the choice and disposal of the speakers. Without hesitation, Dr. Inglis grouped them; with just one look round at those present, and another, well into her own mind, at those not present who could be press-ganged! At last she turned to me and said, 'And you will speak with Miss X. at ——' I was horrified. 'But I must explain,' I said; 'I am quite "new." I don't speak at all. I have never spoken.' I can imagine a hundred people answering my very decided utterance in a hundred different ways. But I cannot imagine anyone but Dr. Inglis answering as she answered. There was just the jolliest, cheeriest laugh and, 'Oh, but you *must* speak.' That was all. And the remarkable thing was that, though I had sworn to myself that I would never utter a word in public without proper training, I did speak that night. It never occurred to me to refuse. Confidence begat confidence. It was during this time of work with Dr. Inglis that I began really to understand and appreciate that wonderful character.

"Another incident runs into my memory, of desperate, agonizing days in Glasgow, when Suffrage was unpopular and the funds in our exchequer were very low. How well I remember writing to Dr. Inglis at the ridiculous hour of two in the morning, that we must get some money, and that I should get certain introductions and do a lecturing tour in New York and try to make Suffrage 'fashionable.' The answer came by return of post, and was deliciously typical. 'My dear, your idea is so absolutely mad that it must be thoroughly sane. Come and talk it over.'

"It was a happiness to work with Dr. Inglis, for her confidence, once given, was complete. There were no petty inquiries or pedantic regulations. 'Do it your own way,' was the one comment on a plan of organization once it was settled.

"Dr. Inglis was one to whom the words 'can't' and 'impossible' really and literally had no meaning; and those who worked with her had to 'unlearn' them, and they did. It did, indeed, seem 'impossible' to leave for India at ten days' notice to carry on negotiations for the Scottish Women's Hospitals and raise an Indian fund, especially when one had been in no way officially or intimately connected with the Hospitals' work. And to be told on the telephone, too, that one 'must' go. That was adorably Dr. Inglis-ish. I laughed with glee at the very ridiculous, fantastic impossibility of the whole thing—and promptly went! And how I looked forward to seeing Dr. Inglis on my return! When she saw me off at Waterloo in 1916, and, still fearfully ignorant of what awaited one, I wailed at the eleventh hour (literally, for we were in the railway carriage), 'But where am I to stay and where am I to go?' 'Don't worry,' said Dr. Inglis, with that sublime faith and optimism of hers; 'they'll put you up and pass you on. Good-bye, my dear. *It will be all right.*' And so it was. But one has missed the telling of it all to her; the hard things and the good things and the dreadfully funny things. For she would have appreciated every bit of it, and entered into every detail."

During the years of that great campaign, Dr. Inglis spoke, pleading the cause of Suffrage, at hundreds of meetings all over the United Kingdom. At one large meeting she had occasion to deal with the problem of the "outcast woman." She referred to the statement once made that no woman would be safe unless this class existed.

Then she said: "If this were true, the price of safety is too high. I, for one, would choose to go down with the minority."

It is difficult to declare which was the more impressive, the silence—one that could be felt—which followed the words, or the burst of applause which came a moment later. But to one onlooker, from the platform, the predominant feeling was wonder at the amazing power of the woman. Without raising her voice, or putting into it any emotion beyond the involuntary momentary break at the beginning of the sentence, she had, by the transparent sincerity of her feeling, conveyed such an impression to that large audience as few there would forget. The subtle response drawn from those hundreds of women to the woman herself, to the personality of the speaker, was for the moment even more real than the outward response given to the idea. More than one woman there that day could have said in the words of the British Tommy, who had heard for the first time the story of Serbia, "It would not be difficult to follow her!"

Chapter IX

THE SCOTTISH WOMEN'S HOSPITALS

"From the first the personality of Dr. Inglis was the main asset in this splendid venture. She continued to be its inspiration to the end."

August, 1914, found many a man and woman unconsciously prepared and ready for the testing time ahead. Elsie Inglis was one of these.

It is interesting to note that Dr. Inglis completed her fiftieth year in the August that war broke out. She started on her great work of the next years with all the vigour and freshness of youth.

In her own words, already quoted, we can describe her at the beginning of the war:

"Her ship was flying over a sunlit sea, the good wind bulging out the canvas. She felt the thrill and excitement of adventure in her veins as she stood at the helm and gazed across the dancing waters.... Joy had done its work, and sorrow and responsibility had come with its stimulating spur, and the ardent delight of battle in a great crusade....

"New powers she had discovered in herself, new responsibilities in the life around her.... She was ready for her 'adventure brave and new.' Rabbi Ben Ezra waited for death to open the gate to it, but to her it seemed that she was in the midst of it now, that 'adventure brave and new' *in which death itself was also to be an adventure....* 'The Power of an Endless Life.' The words thrilled her, not with the prospects of rest, but with the excitement of advance...."

War was declared on August 4. On the 10th the idea of the Scottish Women's Hospitals—hospitals staffed entirely by women—had been mooted at the committee meeting of the Scottish Federation of Women's Suffrage Societies. Once the idea was given expression to, nothing was able to stop its growth. A special Scottish Women's Hospital committee was formed out of members of the Federation and Dr. Inglis's personal friends. Meetings were organized all over the country; an appeal for funds was sent broadcast over Scotland; money began to flow in; the scheme was taken up by the whole body of the N.U.W.S.S.[12] Mrs. Fawcett wrote approvingly. The Scottish

Women's Hospitals Committee at their headquarters in Edinburgh divided up into subcommittees: equipment, uniforms, cars, personnel, and so on. Offers for service came in every day, until soon over 400 names were waiting the choice of the personnel committee. The headquarters offices in 2, St. Andrew Square became a busy hive. Enthusiasm was written on the face of every worker. By the end of November the first fully equipped Unit, under Miss Ivens of Liverpool was on its way to the old Abbey of Royaumont in France. Dr. Alice Hutchison with ten nurses was in Calais working under the Belgian surgeon, Dr. de Page. A second Unit as well equipped as the first was almost ready to start for Serbia. It sailed in the beginning of January, under Dr. Eleanor Soltau, Dr. Inglis herself following in the April of 1915.

But even with all this dispatch, the S.W.H. were not the first Women's Hospital in the field. As early as September, 1914, Dr. Flora Murray and Dr. Louisa Garrett Anderson had taken a Unit, staffed entirely by women, to Paris, where they did excellent work.

Until Dr. Inglis's departure for Serbia, her whole time and strength and boundless energy had been thrown into the building up of the organization of the Scottish Women's Hospitals. She addressed countless meetings all over the Kingdom, making the scheme known and appealing for money, and at the same time her insight and enthusiasm never ceased to be the mainspring of the activity at the office in Edinburgh, where the heart of the Scottish Women's Hospitals was to be found. Miss Mair describes Dr. Inglis during these months thus:

"A certain stir of feeling might be perceptible in the busy hive at the office of organization when a specially energetic visit of the Chief had been paid. Had the impossible been accomplished? If not, why? Who had failed in performance? Take the task from her; give it to another. No excuses in war-time, no weakness to be tolerated—onward, ever onward.

"To those inclined to hesitate, or at least to draw breath occasionally in the course of their heavy work of organizing, raising money, gathering equipment, securing transport, passports, and attending to the other innumerable secretarial affairs connected with so big a task, she showed no weakening pity; the one invariable goad applied was ever, 'it is war-time.' No one must pause, no one must waver; things must simply be done, whether possible or not, and somehow by her inspiration they generally were done. In these days of agonizing stress she appeared as in herself the very embodiment of wireless telegraphy, aeronautic locomotion, with telepathy and divination thrown in—neither time nor space was of account. Puck alone could quite have reached her standard with his engirdling of the earth in forty minutes. Poor limited mortals could but do their best with the terrestrial means at their disposal. Possibly at times their make-weight steadied the brilliant work of their leader."

In a letter to Mrs. Fawcett dated October 4, 1914, she says:

"I can think of nothing except those Units just now; and when one hears of the awful need, one can hardly sit still till they are ready."

FOOTNOTE:

[12] National Union of Women's Suffrage Societies.
ELSIE INGLIS FROM A BUST BY THE SERBIAN SCULPTOR IVAN MESTROVIC

ELSIE INGLIS

FROM A BUST BY THE SERBIAN SCULPTOR IVAN MÉSTROVIC

Chapter X

SERBIA

Serbia in January, 1915, was in a pitiable condition. Three wars following in quick succession had devastated the land. The Austrians, after their defeat at the Battle of the Ridges in October, 1914, had retreated out of the country, leaving behind them filthy hospitals crowded with wounded, Austrian and Serb alike. The whole land has been spoken of as one vast hospital. From this condition of things sprang the scourge of typhus which started in January, 1915, and swept the land. Dr. Soltau and her Unit, arriving in the early part of January, were able to take their place in the battle against this scourge. Their work lay in Kraguevatz, in the north of Serbia, where Dr. Soltau soon had three hospitals under her command.

In April Dr. Soltau contracted diphtheria. Dr. Inglis was wired for, and left for Serbia in the end of April, 1915. She went gaily. There seems no other word to describe her attitude of mind—she was so glad to go. The sufferings of the wounded and dying touched her keenly. It was not want of sympathy with all the awful misery on every hand that made her go with such joy of heart, but rather she was glad from the sense that at last she, personally, would be "where the need was greatest." This had always been her objective.

The Ægean Sea,
"*May 2nd, 1915.*

"Dearest Eva,
"We have had a perfectly glorious voyage from Brindisi to Athens, all yesterday between the coast and the Greek Islands, and then in the Gulf of Corinth. I never remember such a day—all day the sunshine and the beautiful hills, with the clouds capping them, or lying on their slopes, and the blue sky above, and blue sea all round. Then came the most glorious sunset, and when we came up from dinner the sky blazing with stars. We put our chairs back to the last notches, and lay looking at them, till a great yellow moon came up

and flooded the place with light and put the stars out. It was glorious....

"Your loving sister,

"Elsie Inglis."

She landed in Serbia when the epidemic of fever had been almost overcome, and with the long, peaceful summer ahead of her. It is a joy to think of Dr. Inglis all that summer. Her letters are full of buoyancy of spirit. She was keen about everything. She had left behind her a magnificent organization, enthusiastic women in every department, the money flowing in, and the scheme meeting with more and more approval throughout the country. In Serbia she was to find her power of organizing given full scope. She had splendid material in the personnel of the Scottish Women's Hospitals Units under her command. She made many friends—Sir Ralph Paget, Colonel Hunter, Dr. Curcin, Colonel Gentitch, and many others. She was in close touch with, was herself part of, big schemes, a fact which was exhilarating to her. Everything combined to make her happy.

The scheme that eventually took shape was Colonel Hunter's. His idea was to have three "blocking hospitals" in the north of Serbia, which, when the planned autumn offensive of the Serbs took place, would keep all infectious diseases from spreading throughout the country. Innumerable journeys up and down Serbia were taken by Dr. Inglis before the three Scottish Women's Hospitals which were to form this blocking line had been settled, and were working at Valjevo, Lazaravatz, and Mladanovatz. Dr. Alice Hutchison and her Unit, with "the finest canvas hospital ever sent to the Balkans," arrived in Serbia shortly after Dr. Inglis. Dr. Hutchison was sent to Valjevo; Lazaravatz and Mladanovatz were respectively under Dr. Hollway and Dr. McGregor. Dr. Inglis herself took over charge of the fever hospitals in Kraguevatz, working them as one, so that soon there were four efficient Scottish Women's Hospitals in Serbia. The Serbian Government gave Dr. Inglis a free pass over all the railways. She calls herself "extraordinarily lucky" in getting this pass, and writes how greatly she enjoys these journeys, how much of the country she sees during them, and of the interesting people she meets. For the first time in her life she had work to do that needed almost the full stretch of her powers. And deep at the heart of her joy at this time lay her growing love of the Serbs. Something in them appealed to her, something

55

in their heroic weakness satisfied the yearning of her strength to help and protect. She writes glowingly of their soldiers streaming past the Scottish Women's Hospitals at Mladanovatz, massing on the Danube, "their heads held high." Every letter is full of enthusiasm of the country and the people. "God bless her," writes a friend; "it was the last really joyous time she knew."

Later on the Serbs erected a fountain at Mladanovatz in memory of the work done by the Scottish Women's Hospitals in Serbia, and in particular by Dr. Inglis. The opening ceremony took place in the beginning of September. Many people, English and Serbs, were present, and a long letter by Dr. Inglis describes the dedication service.

"A table covered with a white cloth stood in front of the fountain, and on it a silver crucifix, a bowl of water, a long brown candle lighted and stuck in a tumbler full of sand, and two bunches of basil, one fresh and one dried."

At the end of the service the priest gave the bunches of basil to Dr. Inglis. "These are some of the few things," she writes, "which I shall certainly keep always."

The Serbian officer who designed the fountain has contributed to this *Life* the following account of his impressions of Dr. Inglis:

"Already five sad and painful years have gone by since the time that I had the chance and honour of knowing Dr. Elsie Inglis. It is already five years since we erected to her—still in the plenitude of life—a monument. What a prediction! Whence came the inspiration of the great soul who was founder of this monument?

"Oh, great and noble soul, there is yet another monument created in the hearts of the soldiers and Serbian people! And if the pitiless wheel of time crushes the first, the second will survive all that is visible and material.

"One did not need to be long with Dr. Elsie Inglis to see all the grandeur of her soul, her long vision, and her attachment to the Serbs. I was not among those who chanced to pass some months in her company, but even in a few days I soon learnt to recognize her divine nature, and to see her relief in all colours.

"After the second big offensive of Germano-Austrian forces against Serbia in the autumn of 1914, Dr. Elsie Inglis took a great part in working against the various epidemics spread by the invasion in Western Serbia. The

56

significance and tenacity of this time of epidemic was such that only those who witnessed it can understand the great usefulness, devotion, and attachment of its co-workers. A great number of Dr. Inglis's personnel were occupied in coping with it, and with what results!

"The Serbian counter-offensive terminated, provisional peace reigned in Serbia. Six months went by before the last soldier of the enemy left our sacred soil; the second enemy—the great epidemic—has also been arrested and vanquished. The terrors that these two allies brought in their train gradually disappeared, and the sun shone once again for the Little Armed People. Men breathed again, and tired bodies slept. One had the time to think of the great soldiers of the front, as well as those who worked behind the lines. And, indeed, in those great days we knew not who were the more courageous, the more daring, the greater heroes.

"General Headquarters decided to give a tangible recognition to all those who had taken part in this epoch. Among the first thus distinguished were Dr. Elsie Inglis and her hospitals.

"On the proposal of the Director of Sanitation, it was decided to erect a monumental fountain to the memory of Dr. Elsie Inglis and her Scottish Women's Hospitals. This was to be at Mladanovatz, quite close to one of these hospitals, at a few yards' distance from the main railway-line running from Belgrade to Nish, in sight of all the travellers who passed through Serbia.

"It was erected, and bears the inscription:

"In memory of the Scottish Women's Hospitals and their Founder, Dr. Elsie Inglis."

"The object of my letter is not to make known what I have told you; what follows is more important.

"Dr. Inglis was present in person at the unveiling and benediction of the fountain. The idea was to give her a proof of the people's gratitude by erecting an original monument which, in recalling those strenuous days, would combine a value practical and real, solving the question of a pure drinking-water, and cutting off the danger of an epidemic at the root; and also, the impression that she had after visiting a number of fountains in the environs of Mladanovatz and its villages left her no rest (as she said later), and produced in her an idea, long thought over, and eventually expressed in the following conversation:

"'Look here, Captain P——, I have a scheme which absorbs me more and more, and becomes in me a fixed idea. You suffer in Serbia, and are often subject to epidemics, through nothing else but bad water. I have been thinking it over, and would like to ameliorate as much as possible this deplorable state of affairs. I have the intention of addressing an appeal to the people of Great Britain, and asking them to inaugurate a fund which would create the opportunity of constructing in each Serbian village a fountain of good drinking-water. And then, I should return to Serbia, and with you—I hope that you are willing, since you have already built so many of these fountains round about—should go from village to village erecting these fountains. It will be, after the war, my unique and greatest desire to do this for the Serbs.'

"Oh, great friend of Serbia! Thy clear-sighted spirit was to have but a glimpse of one of the most essential necessities of the Serbian people. Thy frail and fragile body has not permitted thee to enjoy the pleasure to which thou hast devoted so much love. For the well-being of this dear people thou hast given thyself entirely, even thy noble life. What a misfortune indeed for us!

"May Heaven send thee eternal peace, so much merited, and so much desired by all those who knew thee, and above all and especially by all those Serbian hearts who have found in thee a great human friend."

Dr. Inglis wrote every week to the committee. In the letters written towards the end of September we are aware of the anxiety about the future which is beginning to make itself felt.

"Last week Austrian aeroplanes were 'announced,' and the authorities evidently believed the report; for the Arsenal was emptied of workmen—and they don't stop work willingly just now. So—as a Serbian officer said to me yesterday—'Serbia is exactly where she was a year ago.' It does seem hard lines on our little Ally....

"Well, as to how this affects us. Sir Ralph was talking about the various possibilities. *As long as the Serbians fight we'll stick to them—retreat if necessary, burning all our stores.* If they are overwhelmed we must escape,

58

probably via Montenegro. Don't worry about us. We won't do anything rash or foolish; and if you will trust us to decide, as we must know most about the situation out here, we'll act rationally."

At last, in November, 1915, the storm broke. Serbia was overrun by Germans, Austrians, and Bulgarians. All her big Allies failed her, "so when her bitter hour of trial came, Serbia stood alone."

The Scottish Women's Hospitals at Mladanovatz, Lazaravatz, and Valjevo had to be evacuated in an incredibly short time. The women from Mladanovatz and Lazaravatz came down to Kraguevatz, where Dr. Inglis was. After a few days they had again to move further south to Krushevatz. From here they broke into two parties, some joining the great retreat and coming home through Albania. The rest stayed behind with Dr. Inglis and Dr. Hollway to nurse the Serbian wounded and prisoners in Krushevatz.

"If the committee could have seen Colonel Gentitch's face when I said to him that we were not going to move again, but that they could count on us just where we stood, I think they would have been touched."

writes Dr. Inglis.

At Krushevatz both Units, Dr. Inglis's and Dr. Hollway's, worked together at the Czar Lazar Hospital under the Serbian Director, Major Nicolitch. It was here they were taken prisoners by the Germans in November.

"These months at Krushevatz were a strange mixture of sorrow and happiness. Was the country really so very beautiful, or was it the contrast to all the misery that made it evident? There was a curious exhilaration in working for those grateful, patient men, and in helping the Director, so loyal to his country and so conscientious in his work, to bring order out of chaos; and yet the unhappiness in the Serbian houses, and the physical wretchedness of those cold, hungry prisoners, lay always like a dead weight on our spirits. Never shall we forget the beauty of the sunrises or the glory of the sunsets, with clear, cold, sunlit days between, and the wonderful starlit nights. But we shall never forget 'the Zoo,'[13] either, or the groans outside when we hid our heads in the blankets to shut out the sound. Nor shall we ever forget the cheeriness or trustfulness of all that hospital, and especially of the officers' ward. We got no news, and we made it a point of honour not to believe a word of the German telegrams posted up in the town. So we lived on rumour—and what rumour! The English at Skoplje, the Italians at Poshega, and the Russians over the Carpathians—we could not believe that Serbia had been sacrificed for nothing. We were convinced it was some deep-laid scheme for weakening the other fronts, and so it was quite natural to hear that the British had taken Belgium and the French were in Metz!"

During this time in Krushevatz Dr. Inglis and the women in her Unit lived and slept in one room. One night an excited message was brought to the door that enemy aircraft was expected soon; everyone was taking refuge in places that were considered safe; would they not come too? For a moment there was a feeling of panic in the room; then Dr. Inglis said, without raising her head from her pillow: "Everyone will do as they like, of course; *I* shall not go anywhere. I am very tired, and bed is a comfortable place to die in." The suspicion of panic subsided; every woman lay down and slept quietly till morning.

The Hon. Mrs. Haverfield was one of the "Scottish women" who stayed behind at Krushevatz. She gives us some memories of Dr. Inglis.

"I think the most abiding recollection I have of our dear Doctor is the expression in her face in the middle of a heavy bombardment by German guns of our hospital at Krushevatz during the autumn of 1915. I was coming across some swampy ground which separated our building from the large barracks called after the good and gentle Czar Lazar of Kosovofanee, when a shell flew over our heads, and burst close by with a deafening roar. The Doctor was coming from the opposite direction; we stood a moment to comment upon the perilous position we were all in. She looked up into my face, and with that smile that nobody who ever knew her could forget, and such a quizzical expression in her blue eyes, said: 'Eve, we are having some experiences now, aren't we?' She and I had often compared notes, and said how we would like to be in the thick of everything—at last we were. I have never seen anyone with greater courage, or anyone who was more unmoved under all circumstances.

"Under our little Doctor bricks had to be made, whether there was straw or not!

"In this same hospital at Krushevatz she had ordered me to get up bathing arrangements for the sick and wounded. There was not a corner in which to make a bath-room, or a can, and only a broken pump 150 yards away across mud and swamp. There was no wood to heat the water, and nothing to heat it in even if we had the wood. I admit I could not achieve the desired arrangement. Elsie took the matter in hand herself, finding I was no use, and in one day had a regular supply of hot water, and baths for the big Magazine, where lay our sick, screened off with sheets, and regular baths were the order of the day from that time forth.

"One never ceased to admire the tireless energy, the resourcefulness, and the complete unselfishness of that little woman who spent herself until the last moment, always in the service of others."

"At last, on the 9th of February, our hospital was emptied.[14] The chronic invalids had been 'put on commission' and sent to their homes. The vast majority of the men had been removed to Hungary, and the few remaining, badly wounded men who would not be fit for months, taken over to the Austrian hospitals.

"On the 11th we were sent north under an Austrian guard with fixed bayonets. Great care was taken that we should not communicate with anyone *en route*. At Belgrade, however, we were put into a waiting-room for the night, and after we had crept into our sleeping-bags we were suddenly roused to speak to a Serbian woman. The kindly Austrian officer in charge of us said she was the wife of a Serbian officer in Krushevatz, and that if we would use only German we might speak to her. She wanted news of her husband. We were able to reassure her. He was getting better—he was in the Gymnasium. 'Vrylo dobra' ('Very well'), she said, holding both our hands. 'Vrylo, vrylo dobra,' we said, looking apprehensively at the officer. But he only laughed. Probably his Serbian, too, was equal to that. That was the last Serbian we spoke to in Serbia, and we left her a little happier. And thus we came to Vienna, where the American Embassy took us over.... When we reached Zurich and found everything much the same as when we disappeared into the silence, our hearts were sick for the people we had left behind us, still waiting and trusting."

Referring to this year of work done for Serbia, Mr. Seton-Watson wrote of Dr. Inglis:

"History will record the name of Elsie Inglis, like that of Lady Paget, as pre-eminent among that band of women who have redeemed for all time the honour of Britain in the Balkans."

We close this chapter on her work in Serbia with tributes to her memory from two of her Serbian friends, Miss Christitch, a well-known journalist, and Lieutenant-Colonel D. C. Popovitch, Professor at the Military Academy in Belgrade.

"Through Dr. Inglis Serbia has come to know Scotland, for I must confess that formerly it was not recognized by our people as a distinctive part of the British Isles. Her name, as that of the Serbian mother from Scotland (Srpska majka iz 'Skotske'), has become legendary throughout the land, and it is not excluded that at a future date popular opinion will claim her as of Serbian descent, although born on foreign soil.

"What appealed to all those with whom Elsie Inglis came in contact in Serbia was her extraordinary sympathy and understanding for the people whose language she could not speak and whose ways and customs must certainly have seemed strange to her. Yet there is no record of misunderstanding between any Serb and Dr. Inglis. Everyone loved her, from the tired peasant women who tramped miles to ask the 'Scottish Doctoress' for advice about their babies to the wounded soldiers whose pain she had alleviated.

"Here I must mention that Dr. Inglis won universal respect in the Serbian medical profession for her skill as a surgeon. During a great number of years past we have had women physicians, and very capable they are too; but, for some reason or other, Serbian women had never specialized in surgery. Hence it was not without scepticism that the male members of the profession received the news that the organizer of the Scottish hospitals was a skilled surgeon. Until Dr. Inglis actually reached Serbia and had performed successfully in their presence, they refused to believe this 'amiable fable,' but from the moment that they had seen her work they altered their opinion, and, to the great joy of our Serbian women, they no longer proclaimed the fact that surgery was not a woman's sphere. This is but one of the services Dr. Inglis has rendered our woman movement in Serbia. To-day we have several active societies working for the enfranchisement of women, and there is no doubt that the record of the Scottish Women's Hospital, organized and equipped by a Suffrage society and entirely run by women, is helping us greatly towards the realization of our goal. It was a cause of delight to our women and of no small surprise to our men that the Scottish Units that came out never had male administrators.

"It is very difficult to say all one would wish about Dr. Inglis's beneficial influence in Serbia in the few lines which I am asked to write. But before I conclude I may be allowed to give my own impression of that remarkable woman. What struck me most in her was her grip of facts in Serbia. I had a long conversation with her at Valjevo in the summer of 1915, before the disaster of the triple enemy onslaught, and while we still believed that the land was safe from a fresh invasion. She spoke of her hopes and plans for the future of Serbia. 'When the war is over,' she said, 'I want to do something lasting for your country. I want to help the women and children; so little has been done for them, and they need so much. I should like to see Serbian qualified nurses and up-to-date women's and children's hospitals. When you will have won your victories you will require all this in order to have a really great and prosperous Serbia.' She certainly meant to return and help us in our reconstruction.

"I saw Dr. Inglis once again several weeks later, at Krushevatz, where she had remained with her Unit to care for the Serbian wounded, notwithstanding the invitation issued her by Army Headquarters to abandon her hospital and return to England. But Dr. Inglis never knew a higher authority than her own conscience. The fact that she remained to face the enemy, although she had no duty to this, her adopted country, was both an inspiration and a consolation to those numerous families who could not leave, and to those of us who, being Serbian, had a duty to remain.

"She left in the spring of 1916, and we never heard of her again in Serbia until the year 1917, when we, in occupied territory, learnt from a German paper that she had died in harness working for the people of her adoption. There was a short and appreciative obituary telling of her movements since she had left us.

"For Serbian women she will remain a model of devotion and self-sacrifice for all time, and we feel that the highest tribute we can pay her is to endeavour, however humbly, to follow in the footsteps of this unassuming, valiant woman."

"My Recollections of Dr. Elsie Inglis.

"I made her acquaintance towards the close of October, 1915, when, as a heavily wounded patient in the Military Hospital of Krushevatz, I became a prisoner, first of the Germans and then of the Austrians.

"The Scottish Women's Hospital Mission, with Dr. Inglis as Head and Mrs. Haverfield as Administrator, had voluntarily become prisoners of the Austrians and Germans, rather than abandon the Serbian sick and wounded they had hitherto cared for. The Mission undertook a most difficult task—that is, the healing of and ministration to the typhus patients, which had already cost the lives of many doctors. But the Scottish women, whose spirit was typified in their leader, Miss Inglis, did not restrict themselves to this department, hastening to assist whenever they could in other departments. In particular, Dr. Elsie Inglis gave help in the surgical ward, and undertook single-handed the charge of a great number of wounded, among whom I was included, and to her devoted sisterly care I am a grateful debtor for my life. She visited me hourly, and not only performed a doctor's duties, but those of a simple nurse, without the slightest reluctance.

"The conditions of Serbian hospitals under the Austrians rendered provisioning one of the most difficult tasks. At the withdrawal of the Serbian Army only the barest necessaries were left behind, and the Austrians gave hardly anything beyond bread, and at times a little meat. The typhus patients were thus dependent almost entirely on the aliments which the Scottish Mission could furnish out of their own means. It was edifying to see how they solved the problem. Every day, their Chief, Dr. Inglis, and Mrs. Haverfield at the head, the nurses off duty, with empty sacks and baskets slung over their shoulders, tramped for miles to the villages around Krushevatz, and after several hours' march through the narrow, muddy paths, returned loaded with cabbages, potatoes, or other vegetables in baskets and sacks, their pockets filled with eggs and apples. Instead of fatigue, joy and satisfaction were evident in their faces, because they were able to do something for their Serbian brothers. I am ever in admiration of these rare women, and never can I forget their watchword: 'Not one of our patients is to be without at least one egg a day, however far we may have to tramp for it.' Such labour, such love towards an almost totally strange nation, is something more than mere humanity; it is the summit of understanding, and the application of real and solid Christian teaching.

"Dr. Inglis cured not only the physical but the moral ills of her wounded patients. Every word she spoke was about the return of our army, and she assured us of final victory. She did not speak thus merely to soothe, for one felt the fire of her indignation against the oppressor, and her love for us and her confidence that our just cause would triumph. I could mention a host of great and small facts in connection with her, enough to fill a book; but, in one word, every move, every thought of the late Dr. Inglis and the members of her Mission breathed affection towards the Serbian soldier and the Serbian nation. The Serbian soldier himself is the best witness to this. One has only to inquire about the Scottish Women's Mission in order to get a short and eloquent comment, which resumes all, and expresses astonishment that he should be asked: 'Of course I know of our sisters from Scotland.' ...

"But the enemy could not succeed in shaking these noble women in their determination and their love for us Serbians. They at last obtained their release, and reached their own country, but, without taking time to rest properly, they at once started to collect fresh stores, and hastened to the assistance of the Serbian Volunteer Corps in the Dobrudja. They returned with the same corps to the Macedonian front, and thence to Serbia once more at the close of last year, in order to come to the aid of the impoverished Serbian people. The fact that Dr. Inglis lost her life after the retreat from Russia is a fresh proof of her devotion to Serbia. The Serbian soldiers mourn her death as that of a mother or sister. The memory of her goodness, self-sacrifice, and unbounded charity, will never leave them as long as they live, and will be handed down as a sacred heritage to their children. The entire Serbian Army and the entire Serbian people weep over the dear departed Dr. Inglis, while erecting a memorial to her in their hearts greater than any of the world's monuments. Glory be to her and the land that gave her birth!

"(*Signed*) Lieut.-Col. Drag. C. Popovitch,
"*Professor at the Military Academy.*

"Belgrade.
"*December 24th, 1919.*"

Dr. Inglis was at home from February to August, 1916. Besides her

65

work as chairman of the committee for Kossovo Day, she was occupied in many other ways. She paid a visit of inspection for the Scottish Women's Hospitals Committee to their Unit in Corsica, reporting in person to them on her return in her usual clear and masterly way on the work being done there. She worked hard to get permission for the Scottish Women's Hospitals to send a Unit to Mesopotamia, where certainly the need was great. It has been said of her that, "like Douglas of old, she flung herself where the battle raged most fiercely, always claiming and at last obtaining permission to set up her hospitals where the obstacles were greatest and the dangers most acute."

It was not the fault of the Scottish Women's Hospitals that their standard was not found flying in Mesopotamia.

During the time she was at home, in the intervals of her other activities, she spoke at many meetings, telling of the work of the Scottish Women's Hospitals. At these meetings she would speak for an hour or more of the year's work in Serbia without mentioning herself. She had the delightful power of telling a story without bringing in the personal note. Often at the end of a meeting her friends would be asked by members of the audience if Dr. Inglis had not been in Serbia herself. On being assured that she had, they would reply incredulously, "But she never mentioned herself at all!"

The Honorary Secretary of the Clapham High School Old Girls' Society wrote, after Dr. Inglis's death, describing one of these meetings:

"In June, 1916, Dr. Inglis came to our annual commemoration meeting and spoke to us of Serbia. None of those who were present will, I think, ever forget that afternoon, and the almost magical inspiration of her personality. Behind her simple narrative (from which her own part in the great deeds of which she told seemed so small that to many of us it was a revelation to learn later what that part had been) lay a spiritual force which left no one in the audience untouched. We feel that we should like to express our gratitude for that afternoon in our lives, as well as our admiration of her gallant life and death."

The door to Mesopotamia being still kept closed, Dr. Inglis, in August, 1916, went to Russia as C.M.O. of a magnificently equipped Unit which was being sent to the help of the Jugo-Slavs by the Scottish Women's Hospitals.

A few days before she left Dr. Inglis went to Leven, on the Fifeshire coast of Scotland, where many of her relatives were gathered, to say farewell. The photograph given here was taken at this time.

FOOTNOTES:

[13] The name the nurses gave the huge building they had converted into a hospital.

[14] Dr. Inglis's report.

ELSIE INGLIS TAKEN IN AUGUST, 1916, JUST BEFORE SHE LEFT FOR RUSSIA

ELSIE INGLIS

TAKEN IN AUGUST, 1916, JUST BEFORE SHE LEFT FOR RUSSIA

Chapter XI

RUSSIA

"For a clear understanding and appreciation of subsequent events affecting the relations between Dr. Inglis and the Serb division, a brief account of its genesis may be given here.

"The division consisted mainly of Serbo-Croats and Slovenes—namely, Serbs who, as subjects of Austria-Hungary, were obliged to serve in the Austrian Army. Nearly all of these men had been taken prisoners by the Russians, or, perhaps more correctly, had voluntarily surrendered to the Russians rather than fight for the enemies of their co-nationals. In May, 1915, a considerable number of these Austro-Serbs volunteered for service with the Serbian Army, and by arrangement with the Russian Government, who gave them their freedom, they were transported to Serbia. After the entry of Bulgaria into the war it was no longer possible to send them to Serbia, and 2,000 were left behind at Odessa. The number of these volunteers increased, however, to such an extent that, by permission of the Serbian Government, Serbian officers from Corfu were sent over to organize them into a military unit for service with the Russian Army. By May, 1916, a first division was formed under the command of the Serb Colonel, Colonel Hadjitch, and later a second division under General Zivkovitch. It was to the first division that the Scottish Women's Hospitals and Transport were to be attached.

"The Unit mustered at Liverpool on August 29, and left for Archangel on the following day. It consisted of a personnel of seventy-five and three doctors, with Dr. Elsie Inglis C.M.O."[15]

A member of the staff describes the journey:

"Our Unit left Liverpool for Russia on August 31, 1916; like the Israelites of old, we went out not knowing exactly where we were bound for. We knew only that we had to join the Serbian division of the Russian Army, but where that Division was or how we were to get there we could not tell. We were seventy-five all told, with 50 tons of equipment and sixteen automobiles. We had a special transport, and after nine days over the North Sea we arrived at Archangel.

"From Archangel we were entrained for Russia, and sent down via Moscow to Odessa, receiving there further instructions to proceed to the Roumanian front, where our Serbs were in action.

"We were fourteen days altogether in the train. I remember Dr. Inglis, during those long days on the journey, playing patience, calm and serene, or losing her own patience when the train was stopped and *would* not go on. Out she would go, and address the Russian officials in strenuous, nervous British—it was often effective. One of our interpreters heard one stationmaster saying: 'There is a great row going on here, and there will be trouble to-morrow if this train isn't got through.'

"At Reni we were embarked on a steamer and barges, and sent down the Danube to a place called Cernavoda, where once more we were disembarked, and proceeded by train and motor to Medjidia, where our first hospital was established in a large barracks on the top of a hill above the town, an excellent mark for enemy aeroplanes. The hospital was ready for wounded two days after our arrival; until then it was a dirty empty building, yet the wounded were received in it some forty-eight hours after our arrival. It was a notable achievement, but for Dr. Inglis obstacles and difficulties were placed in her path for the purpose of being overcome; if the mountains of Mahomet *would* not move, she *removed* them!

"In connection with the establishment of these field hospitals I have vivid recollections of her. The great empty upper floor of the barracks at Medjidia, seventy-five of us all in the one room. The lines of camp beds. Dr. Inglis and her officers in one corner; and how quietly in all the noise and hubbub she went to bed and slept. I remember how I had to waken her when certain officials came on the night of our arrival to ask when we would be ready for the wounded. 'Say to-morrow,' she said, and slept again!

"'It's a wonder she did not say *now*,' one of my fellow-officers remarked!

"We were equipped for two field hospitals of 100 beds each, and our second hospital was established close to the firing-line at Bulbulmic. We were at Bulbulmic and Medjidia only some three weeks when we had to retreat."

Three weeks of strenuous work at these two places ended in a sudden evacuation and retreat—Hospital B and the Transport got separated from Hospital A. We can only, of course, follow the fortunes of Hospital A, which was directly under Dr. Inglis.

The night of the retreat is made vivid for us by Dr. Inglis:

"The station was a curious sight that night. The flight was beginning. A crowd of people was collected at one end with boxes and bundles and children. One little boy was lying on a doorstep asleep, and against the wall farther on lay a row of soldiers. On the bench to the right, under the light, was a doctor in his white overall, stretched out sound asleep between the two rushes of work at the station dressing-room; and a Roumanian officer talked to me of Glasgow, where he had once been invited out to dinner, so he had seen the British 'custims.' It was good to feel those British customs were still going quietly on, whatever was happening here—breakfasts coming regularly, hot water for baths, and everything as it should be. It was probably absurd, but it came like a great wave of comfort to feel that Britain was there, quiet, strong, and invincible, behind everything and everybody."

A member of the Unit also gives us details:[16]

"I went twice down to the station with baggage in the evening, a perilous journey in rickety carts through pitch darkness over roads (?) crammed with troops and refugees, which were lit up periodically by the most amazing green lightning I have ever seen, and the roar and flash of the guns was incessant. At the station no lights were allowed because of enemy aircraft, but the place was illuminated here and there by the camp fires of a new Siberian division which had just arrived. Picked troops these, and magnificent men.

"We wrestled with the baggage until 2 a.m., and went back to the hospital in one of our own cars. Our orderly came in almost in tears. Her cart had twice turned over completely on its way to the station; so on arrival she had hastened to Dr. Inglis with a tale of woe and a scratched face. Dr. Inglis said: 'That's right, dear child, that's right, *stick* to the equipment,' which may very well be described as the motto of the Unit these days!...

"The majority of the Unit are to go to Galatz by train with Dr. Corbett; the rest (self included) are to go by road with Dr. Inglis, and work with the army as a clearing station.

"On the morning of October 22 the train party got off as quick as possible, and about 4 p.m. a big lorry came for our equipment. We loaded it, seven of us mounted on the top, and the rest went in two of our own cars. The scene was really intensely comic. Seven Scottish women balanced precariously on the pile of luggage; a Serbian doctor with whom Dr. Inglis is to travel standing alongside in an hysterical condition, imploring us to hurry, telling us the Bulgarians were as good as in the town already; Dr. Inglis, quite unmoved, demanding the whereabouts of the Ludgate boiler; somebody arriving at the last minute with a huge open barrel of treacle, which, of course, could not possibly be left to a German. Oh dear! how we laughed!"

Dr. Inglis would never allow the Sunday service to be missed if it was at all possible to hold it.[17] Miss Onslow tells us how she seized a seeming opportunity even on this Sunday of so many dangers to make ready for the service.

"*Medjidia.*—Sunday was the day on which we began our retreat from the Dobrudja. We spent most of the morning going to and from the station—a place almost impossible to enter or leave on account of the refugees, their carts and animals, and the army, which was on the move, blocking all the approaches—transporting sick members of the Unit and some equipment which had still to be put on the train, and only my touring car and one ambulance with which to do the work. Dr. Inglis had been at the station until the early hours of the morning, but nevertheless superintended everything that was being done both at the train and up at the hospital.

"Towards noon a Serbian officer brought in a report that things were not as bad for the moment as they expected. Whereupon the Doctor immediately gave orders to prepare the room for service at 4 o'clock that afternoon! And she began revolving plans for immediate work in Medjidia. But, alas! the good news was a false report—the enemy was rushing onwards. The Russian lorry came for the personal baggage and any remaining equipment which had not gone by train; and it, piled high with luggage and some of the staff, left at 3, the remainder of us going in the ambulance and my car. Dr. Inglis came in my car, and I had the honour of driving our dear Doctor nearly all the time, and am the only member of the Unit who was with her the whole time of the retreat from Medjidia until we reached the Danube at Harshova."

The four days of the Dobrudja retreat from October 22nd to 26th were days of horror for all who took part in it, not least for Dr. Inglis and the members of her Units. "At first we passed a few carts, then at some distance more and more, till we found ourselves in an unending procession of peasants with all their worldly goods piled on those vehicles.... This procession seemed difficult to pass, but as time went on, added to it, came the Roumanian army retreating—hundreds of guns, cavalry, infantry, ambulances, Red Cross carts, motor-kitchens, and wounded on foot—a most extraordinary scene. The night was inky black; the only lights were our own head-lights and those of the ambulance behind us, but they revealed a sad and never-to-be-forgotten picture. Our driver was quite wonderful; she sat unmoved, often for half an hour at a time. There was a block, and we had to wait while the yelling, frantic mob did what they could to get into some sort of order; then we would move on for ten minutes, and then stop again; it was like a dream or a play; it certainly was a tragedy. No one spoke; we just waited and watched it all; to us it was a spectacle, to these poor homeless people it was a terrible reality."[18]

At 11.30 that Sunday night Dr. Inglis and the party with her arrived at Caramarat. The straw beds and the fairytale dinner, and the cheery voice of Dr. Inglis calling them to partake of it, will never be forgotten by these Scottish women.

On arrival at Caramarat Dr. Inglis had asked for a room for her Unit and "a good meat meal." She was told a room was waiting for them, but a good meal was an impossibility; the town had been evacuated; there had been no food to be got for days.

"Though it was only a bare room with straw in heaps on the floor and green blankets to wrap ourselves in, to cold, shivering beings like ourselves it seemed all that heart could desire.... Never shall I forget the delight of lying down on the straw, the dry warm blanket rolled round me. Then a most wonderful thing happened—the door opened and several soldiers entered with the most beautiful meal I ever ate. It was like a fairytale. Where did it come from? The lovely soup—the real Russian *borsh*—and roast turkey and plenty of bread and *chi*. We ate like wolves, and I can remember so distinctly sitting up in my straw nest, with my blanket round me, and hearing Dr. Inglis's cheery voice saying, 'Isn't this better than having to start and cook a meal?' She was the most extraordinary person; when she said she must have a thing, she got it, and it was never for herself, always for others."[19]

They started again early on Monday morning, and after another day of adventures slept that night in the open air beside a river.

"Cushions were brought from the cars and all the rugs we could find, and soon we were sitting round the fire waiting for the water to boil for our tea, and a more delightful merry meal could not be imagined. We all told our experiences of the day, and Dr. Inglis said: 'But this is the best of all; it is just like a fairytale.' And so it was; for as we looked there were groups of soldiers holding their horses, standing motionless, staring at us; we saw them only through the wood-smoke. The fire attracted them, and they came to see what it could mean. Seeing nine women laughing and chatting, alone and within earshot of the guns, the distant sky-line red with the enemy's doings, was more than they could understand. They did not speak, but quietly went away as they had come.... Rolled in our blankets, with the warmth of the fire making us feel drowsy, our chatter gradually ceased, and we slept as only a day in the open air can make one sleep."

Another two days of continued retreat, and the different parties of Scottish women arrived at places of safety.

"Thus we all came through the Dobrudja retreat. We had only been one month in Roumania, but we seemed to have lived a lifetime between the 22nd and 26th of October, 1916." In a letter to the Committee Dr. Inglis says of the Unit: "They worked magnificently at Medjidia, and took the retreat in a very joyous, indomitable way. One cannot say they were plucky, because I don't think it ever entered their heads to be afraid."

Finally the scattered members of the Unit joined forces again at Braila, where Dr. Inglis opened a hospital.

During the time at Braila Dr. Inglis wrote to her relations. The letter is dated Reni, where she had gone for a few days.

"Reni,
"*October 28th, 1916.*

"Dearest Amy,

"Just a line to say I am all right. Four weeks to-morrow since we reached Medjidia and began our hospital. We evacuated it in three weeks, and here we are all back on the frontier.... Such a time it has been, Amy dear; you cannot imagine what war is just behind the lines. And in a retreat....

"Our second retreat—and almost to the same day. We evacuated Kraguevatz on the 25th of October last year. We evacuated Medjidia on the 22nd this year. On the 25th this year we were working in a Russian dressing-station at Harshova, and were moved on in the evening. We arrived at Braila to find 11,000 wounded and seven doctors, only one of them a surgeon.

"Boat come—must stop—am going back to Braila to do surgery. Have sent every trained person there.

"Ever, you dear, dear people,

"Your loving sister,

"Elsie.

"We have had lots of exciting things too—and amusing things—and *good* things."

Two further retreats had, however, to be experienced by Dr. Inglis and her Unit before they could settle down to steady work. The three retreats took place in the following order:

Sunday, October 22nd.—Retreated from Medjidia.

October 25th.—Arrived at Braila. Worked there till December 3rd.

December 3rd.—Retreated to Galatz, where very strenuous work awaited them.

January 4th.—Retreated to Reni.

August, 1917.—Left Reni, and rejoined the Serb division at Hadji Abdul.

The work during the above period, from October 25th, 1916, to August, 1917, was done for the Russians and Roumanians. As soon as it was possible, Dr. Inglis joined the Serb division in the end of August, 1917.

"Dr. Inglis was still working in Reni when the Russian Revolution broke out in March.[20] The spirit of unrest and indiscipline, which manifested itself among the troops, spread also to the hospitals, and a Russian doctor reported that in the other hospitals the patients had their own committees, which fixed the hours for meals and doctors' visits and made hospital discipline impossible. But there was no sign of this under Dr. Inglis's kindly but firm rule. Without relaxing disciplinary measures, she did all in her

75

power to keep the patients happy and contented; and as the Russian Easter drew near, she bought four ikons to be put up in the wards, that the men might feel more at home. The result of this kindly thought was a charming Easter letter written by the patients—

"To the Much-honoured Elsie Maud, the Daughter of John.

"The wounded and sick soldiers from all parts of the army and fleet of great free Russia, who are now for healing in the hospital which you command, penetrated with a feeling of sincere respect, feel it their much-desired duty, to-day, on the day of the feast of Holy Easter, to express to you our deep reverence to you, the doctor warmly loved by all, and also to your honoured personnel of women. We wish also to express our sincere gratitude for all the care and attention bestowed on us, and we bow low before the tireless and wonderful work of yourself and your personnel, which we see every day directed towards the good of the soldiers allied to your country.... May England live!

"(*Signed*) The Russian Citizen Soldiers."

We cannot be too grateful to one member of the Unit who, in her impressions of Dr. Inglis, has given us a picture of her during these months in Russia that will live:

"I think so much stress has been laid, by those who worked under her, on the leader who said there was no such word as 'can't' in the dictionary, that the extraordinarily lovable personality that lay at the root of her leadership is in danger of being obscured. I do not mean by this that we all had a romantic affection for her. Her influence was of a much finer quality just because she never dragged in the personal element. She was the embodiment of so much, and achieved more in her subordinates, just because she had never to depend for their loyalty on the limits of an admired personality.

"There is no one I should less like to hear described as 'popular.' No one had less an easy power of endearing herself at first sight to those with whom she came in contact—at least, in the relations of the Unit. The first impression, as has been repeated over and over again, was always one of great strength and singleness of purpose, but all those fine qualities with which the general public is, quite rightly, ready to credit her had their roots in a serenity and gentleness of spirit which that same public has had all too little opportunity to realize. Her Unit itself realized it slowly enough. They obeyed at first because she was stronger than they, only later because she was finer and better.

"You know it was not, at least, an easy job to win the best kind of service from a mixed lot of women, the trained members of which had never worked under a woman before, and were ready with their very narrow outlook to seize on any and every opportunity for criticism. There was much opposition, more or less grumblingly expressed at first. No one hesitated to do what she was told—impossible with Dr. Inglis as a chief—but it was grudgingly done. In the end it was all for the best. If she had been the kind of person who took trouble to rouse an easy personal enthusiasm, the whole thing would have fallen to pieces at the first stress of work; on the other hand, if she had never inspired more than respect, she would never have won the quality of service she succeeded in winning. The really mean-spirited were loyal just so long as she was present because she daunted them, and Dr. Inglis's disapproval was most certainly a thing to be avoided. But the great majority, whatever their personal views, were quickly ready to recognize her authority as springing from no hasty impulse, but from a finely consistent discipline of thought.

"We were really lucky in having the retreat at the beginning of the work. It helped the Unit to realize how complete was the radical confidence they felt in her. I think her extraordinary love of justice was next impressed upon them. It took the sting out of every personal grievance, and was so almost passionately sincere it hardly seemed to matter if the verdict went against you. Her selflessness was an example, and often enough a reproach, to every one of us, and to go to her in any personal difficulty was such a revelation of sympathy and understanding as shed a light on those less obvious qualities that really made all she achieved possible.

"People have often come to me and said casually, 'Oh yes, Dr. Inglis was a very charming woman, wasn't she?' And I have felt sorely tempted to say rather snappishly, 'No, she wasn't.' Only they wouldn't have understood.

It is because their 'charming' goes into the same category as my 'popular.'

"I am afraid you will hardly have anticipated such an outburst; the difficulty is, indeed, to know where to stop. For what could I not say of the way her patients adored her—the countless little unerring things she did and said which just kept us going, when things were unusually depressing, or the Unit unusually weary and homesick; the really good moments when one won the generous appreciation that was so well worth the winning; and last—if I may strike this note—her endless personal kindness to me."

The following letter to her sister, Mrs. Simson, reveals something of the lovable personality of Elsie Inglis. The nephew to whom it refers was wounded in the eye at the battle of Gaza, and died a fortnight before she did.

"Odessa,
"*June 24th, 1917.*

"Dearest, Dearest Amy,

"Eve's letter came yesterday about Jim, and though I start at seven to-morrow morning for Reni, I must write to you, dear, before I go. Though what one can say I don't know. One sees these awful doings all round one, but it strikes right home when one thinks of *Jim*. Thank God he is still with us. The dear, dear boy! I suppose he is home by now. And anyhow he won't be going out again for some time. We are all learning much from this war, and I know —— will say it is all our own faults, but I am not sure that the theory that it is part of the long struggle between good and evil does not appeal more to my mind. We are just here in it, and whatever we suffer and whatever we lose, it is for the right we are standing.... It is all terrible and awful, and I don't believe we can disentangle it all in our minds just now. The only thing is just to go on doing one's bit.... Miss Henderson is taking home with her to-day a Serb officer, quite blind, shot right through behind his eyes, to place him somewhere where he can be trained. I heard of him just after I had read Eve's letter, and I nearly cried. He wasn't just a case at that minute, with my thoughts full of Jim. Dear old Jim! Give him my love, and tell him I'm *proud of him*. And how splendidly the regiment did, and how they suffered!

"Ever your loving sister,
"Elsie Maud Inglis."

Another of her Unit, who worked with Dr. Inglis not only during the year in Russia, but through much of the strenuous campaign for the Suffrage, gives us these remembrances:

"Our Last Communion.

"'He that dwelleth in the secret place of the Most High shall abide under the shadow of the Almighty.'

"Dearer to me even than the memory of those outstanding qualities of great-hearted initiative, courage, and determination which helped to make Dr. Elsie Inglis one of the great personalities of her age is the remembrance of certain moments when, in the intimacy of close fellowship during my term of office with her on active service, I caught glimpses of that simple, sublime faith by which she lived and in which she died.

"One of my most precious possessions is the Bible Dr. Inglis read from when conducting the service held on Sunday in the saloon of the transport which took our Unit out to Archangel. The whole scene comes back so vividly! The silent, listening lines of the girls on either hand—Hospital grey and Transport khaki; in the centre, standing before the Union Jack-covered desk, the figure of our dear Chief, and her clear, calm voice—'He that dwelleth in the secret place of the Most High.' One felt that such a 'secret place' was indeed the abode of her serene spirit, and that there she found that steadfastness of purpose which never wavered, and the strength by which she exercised, not only the gracious qualities of love, but those sterner ones of ruthlessness and implacability which are among the essentials of leadership.

"Dr. Inglis was a philosopher in the calm way in which she took the vicissitudes of life. It was only when her judgment, in regard to the work she was engaged in, was crossed that you became aware of her ruthlessness—her *wonderful* ruthlessness! I can find no better adjective. This quality of hers, perhaps more than any other, drew out my admiration and respect. Slowly it was borne in on those who worked with her that under no circumstances whatever would she fail the cause for which she was working, or those who had chosen to follow her.

"Another remembrance! By the banks of the Danube at Reni, where at night the searchlight of the enemy used to play upon our camp, in the tent erected by the girls for the service, with the little altar simply and beautifully decorated by the nurses' loving hands, I see her kneeling beside me wrapt in a deep meditation, from which I ventured to rouse her, as the Chaplain came towards her with the sacred Bread and Wine. Looking back, it seems to me that even then her soul was reaching out beyond this present consciousness:

"'Here in the body pent, Absent from Him I roam.'

The look on her face was the look of those who hold high Communion. So 'in remembrance' we ate and drank of the same Bread and the same Cup. Even as I write these words remembrance comes again, and I know that, although her bodily presence is removed, her spirit is in communion still."

FOOTNOTES:

[15] *A History of the Scottish Women's Hospitals.* Hodder and Stoughton. 7s. 6d.

[16] *With the Scottish Nurses in Roumania*, by Yvonne Fitzroy.

[17] We recall her great-uncle William Money's strict observance of the Sabbath.

[18] "The Dobrudja Retreat," *Blackwood*, March, 1918.

[19] *Blackwood*, March, 1918.

[20] *A History of the Scottish Women's Hospitals.*

Chapter XII

"IF YOU WANT US HOME, GET *THEM* OUT"

Through the summer months of 1917 Dr. Inglis had been working to get the Serbian division to which her Unit was attached out of Russia. They were in an unenviable position. The disorganization of the Russian Army made the authorities anxious to keep the Serbian division there "to stiffen the Russians." The Serb Command realized, on the other hand, that no effective stand at that time would be made by the Russians, and that to send the Serbs into action would be to expose them to another disaster such as had overtaken them in the Dobrudja. In the battle of the Dobrudja the Serb division had gone into the fight 14,000 strong; they were in the centre, with the Roumanians on the left and the Russians on the right. The Roumanians and Russians broke, and the Serbs, who had fought for twenty-four hours on two fronts, came out with only 4,000 men. Further slaughter such as this would have been the fate of the Serbian division if left in Russia.

"The men want to fight," said General Zivkovitch to Dr. Inglis; "they are not cowards, but it goes to my heart to send them to their death like this."

In July there had seemed to be a hope of the division being liberated and sent via Archangel to another front; however, later the decision of the Russian Headquarters was definitely stated. The Serbs were to be kept on the Roumanian front. "The Serb Staff were powerless in the matter, and entirely dependent on the good offices of the British Government for effecting their release."

Into this difficult situation Dr. Inglis descended, and brought to bear on it all the force of which she was capable. The whole story of her achievement is told in *A History of the Scottish Women's Hospitals*, in those chapters that are written by Miss Edith Palliser. Here we can only refer to the message Dr. Inglis sent to the Foreign Office through Sir George Buchanan, British Ambassador at Petrograd, giving her own clear views on the position and affirming that "In any event the Scottish Women's Hospitals will stand by the Serbian division, and will accompany them if they go to Roumania."

At the end of the month of August the Unit, leaving Reni, rejoined the Serb division at Hadji-Abdul, a little village midway between Reni and Belgrade.

Dr. Inglis described it as a

"lovely place ... and we have a perfectly lovely camping-ground among the trees. The division is hidden away wonderfully under the trees, and at first they were very loath to let us pitch our big tents, that could not be so thoroughly hidden; but I was quite bent on letting them see what a nice hospital you had sent out, so I managed to get it pitched, and they are so pleased with us. They bring everybody—Russian Generals, Roumanian Military Attachés and Ministers—to see it, and they are quite content because our painted canvas looks like the roofs of ordinary houses."

"There was a constant rumour of a 'grand offensive' to be undertaken on the Roumanian front, which Dr. Inglis, though extremely sceptical of any offensive on a large scale, made every preparation to meet.

"The London Committee had cabled to Dr. Inglis in the month of August advising the withdrawal of the Unit, but leaving the decision in her hands, to which she replied:

"'I am grateful to you for leaving decision in my hands. I will come with the division.'

"Following upon this cable came a letter, in which she emphasized her reasons for remaining:

"'If there were a disaster we should none of us ever forgive ourselves if we had left. We *must* stand by. If you want us home, get *them* out.'"

Orders and counter-orders for the release of the division were incessant, and on their release depended, as we have seen, the home-coming of the Unit.

"The London Units Committee had feared greatly for the fate of the Unit if, as seemed probable, the Serb division was not able to leave Russia, and on November 9 approached the Hon. H. Nicholson at the War Department of the Foreign Office, who assured them that the Unit would be quite safe with the Serbs, who were well disciplined and devoted to Dr. Inglis. At that moment he thought it would be most unsafe for the Unit to leave the Serbs and to try to come home overland.

"Mr. Nicholson expressed the opinion that the Committee would never persuade Dr. Inglis to leave her Serbs, and added: 'I cannot express to you our admiration here for Dr. Inglis and the work your Units have done.'"[21]

At last the release of the division was effected, and on November 14 a cable was received by the Committee from Dr. Inglis from Archangel announcing her departure:

"On our way home. Everything satisfactory, and all well except me."

This was the first intimation the London Committee had received that Dr. Inglis was ill.

She arrived at Newcastle on Friday, November 23, bringing her Unit and the Serbian division with her. A great gale was blowing in the river, and they were unable to land until Sunday. Dr. Inglis had been very ill during the whole voyage, but on the Sunday afternoon she came on deck, and stood for half an hour whilst the officers of the Serbian division took leave of her.

"It was a wonderful example of her courage and fortitude. She stood unsupported—a splendid figure of quiet dignity, her face ashen and drawn like a mask, dressed in her worn uniform coat, with the faded ribbons, that had seen such good service. As the officers kissed her hand, she said to each of them a few words, accompanied with her wonderful smile."

She had stood through the summer months in Russia, an indomitable little figure, refusing to leave, until she had got ships for the remnant of the Serbian division, and then, with her Serbs and her Unit around her, she landed on the shores of England, to die.

FOOTNOTE:

[21] *A History of The Scottish Women's Hospitals.*

83

Chapter XIII

"THE NEW WORK" AND MEMORIES

"Never knew I a braver going Never read I of one....

"You faced the shadow with all tenderest words of love for all of us, but with not one selfish syllable on your lips."[22]

Dr. Inglis was brought on shore on Sunday evening, and a room was taken for her in the Station Hotel at Newcastle.

"The victory over Death has begun when the fear of death is destroyed."

She had been dying by inches for months. She had fought Death in Russia; she had fought him through all the long voyage. It was a strange warfare. For he was not to be stayed. Irresistible, majestic, wonderful, he took his toll—and yet she remained untouched by him! With unclouded vision, undimmed faith, and undaunted courage, serene and triumphant, in the last, *she passed him by*.

There was no fear in that room on the evening that Elsie Inglis "went forth."

Dr. Ethel Williams writes of her in November, 1919: "The demonstration of serenity of spirit and courage during Dr. Inglis's last illness was so wonderful that it has dwelt with me ever since. At first one felt that she did not in the least grasp the seriousness of her condition, but very soon one realized that she was just meeting fresh events with the same fearlessness and serenity of spirit as she had met the uncertainties and difficulties of life."

One of her nieces was with her the whole of that last day. After Dr. Ethel Williams's visit, when for the first time Elsie Inglis realized that the last circle of her work on earth was complete, she said to her niece, "It is grand to think of beginning a new work over there!"

By the evening her sisters were with her. To the very last her mind was clear, her spirit dominant. Her confident "I know," in response to every thought and word of comfort offered to her, was the outward expression of her inward State of Faith.

What made her passing so mighty and full of triumph? Surely it was the "Power of an Endless Life," that idea to which she had committed herself years ago as she had stood at the open grave where the first seemingly hopeless good-bye had been said. The Power of that Endless Life, the Life of Christ, carried her forward on its mighty current into the New Region shut out from our view, but where the Life is still the same.

We have watched through these pages the widening circles of Elsie Inglis's life. Her medical profession, The Hospice, the Women's Movement, the Scottish Women's Hospitals, Serbia, her achievements in Russia—these we know of; the work which has been given to her now is beyond our knowledge; but "we look after her with love and admiration, and know that somewhere, just out of sight, she is still working in her own keen way," circle after circle of service widening out in endless joyousness.

On Thursday, November 29, St. Giles's Cathedral in Edinburgh was filled with a great congregation, assembled to do honour to the memory of Elsie Inglis. She was buried with military honours. At the end of the service the Hallelujah Chorus was played, and after the Last Post the buglers of the Royal Scots rang out the Réveillé. From the door of the Cathedral to the Dean Cemetery the streets were lined with people waiting to see her pass. "Dr. Inglis was buried with marks of respect and recognition which make that passing stand alone in the history of the last rites of any of her fellow-citizens." It was not a funeral, but a triumph. "What a triumphal home-coming she had!" said one friend. And another wrote: "How glorious the service was yesterday! I don't know if you intended it, but one impression was uppermost in my mind, which became more distinct after I left, until by evening it stood out clear and strong. The note of *Victory*. I had a curious impression that her spirit was there, just before it passed on to larger spheres, and that it was glad. I felt I must tell you. I wonder if you felt it too. The note of Victory was bigger than the war. The Soul triumphant passing on. The Réveillé expressed it."

THE HIGH STREET, EDINBURGH, LOOKING TOWARDS ST. GILES

Photo by D. Scott

THE HIGH STREET, EDINBURGH, LOOKING TOWARDS ST. GILES

In the two Memorial Services held to commemorate Dr. Inglis, one in St. Giles's Cathedral and the other in St. Margaret's, Westminster, a week later, the whole nation and all the interests of her life were represented.

Royalty was represented, the Foreign Office, the War Office, the Admiralty, different bodies of women workers, the Suffrage cause, the Medical world, the Serbians, and—the children.

Scores of "her children" were in St. Giles's, scattered through the congregation; in the crowds who lined the streets, they were seen hanging on to their mothers' skirts; and they were round the open grave in the Dean Cemetery. These were the children of the wynds and closes of the High Street, some of them bearing her name, "Elsie Maud," to whom she had never been too tired or too busy to respond when they needed her medical help or when "they waved to her across the street."

"The estimate of a life of such throbbing energy, the summing up of achievement and influence in due proportion—these belong to a future day. But we are wholly justified in doing honour to the memory of a woman whose personality won the heart of an entire brave nation, and of whom one of the gallant Serbian officers who bore her body to the grave said, with simple earnestness: 'We would almost rather have lost a battle than lost her!'"[23]

"Alongside the wider public loss, the full and noble public recognition, there stands in the shadow the unspoken sorrow of her Unit. The price has been paid, and paid as Dr. Inglis herself would have wished it, on the high completion of a chapter in her work, but we stand bowed before the knowledge of how profound and how selfless was that surrender. Month after month her courage and her endurance never flagged. Daily and hourly, in the very agony of suffering and death, she gave her life by inches. Sad and more difficult though the road must seem to us now, our privilege has been a proud one: to have served and worked with her, to have known the unfailing

86

support of her strength and sympathy, and, best of all, to be permitted to preserve through life the memory and the stimulus of a supreme ideal."[24]

"So passes the soul of a very gallant woman. Living, she spent herself lavishly for humanity. Dying, she joins the great unseen army of Happy Warriors, who as they pass on fling to the ranks behind a torch which, pray God, may never become a cold and lifeless thing."[25]

FOOTNOTES:

[22] In a letter written to his son after his death: see *Life beyond Death*, by Minot Judson Savage.

[23] The Very Rev. Wallace Williamson.

[24] Miss Yvonne Fitzroy in *With the Scottish Nurses in Roumania.*

[25] A writer in the *Sunday Times.*

BIBLIOGRAPHY

[The following books will be found of value by those whose interest may have been awakened by these pages to desire to know more of the career chosen by Elsie Inglis, and to gain an entrance into the lives of other men and women who have followed the medical profession both at home and abroad.—Ed.]

The Problem of Creation. By J. E. Mercer, Bp. S.P.C.K.

Pioneers of Progress (Men of Science). Edited by S. Chapman, M.A., D.Sc. S.P.C.K.

God and the World. By Canon A. W. Robinson. S.P.C.K.

The Natural and Supernatural in Science and Religion. By J. M. Wilson. S.P.C.K.

The Mystery of Life. By J. E. Mercer, Bp. S.P.C.K.

Where Science and Religion Meet. By Scott Palmer. S.P.C.K.

The Natural Law in the Spiritual World. By Henry Drummond. Hodder and Stoughton.

Introduction to Science. By Prof. J. A. Thomson. Williams and Norgate.

The Warder of Life. By Prof. J. A. Thomson. Melrose and Sons.

Secrets of Animal Life. By Prof. J. A. Thomson. Melrose and Sons.

Darwinism and Human Life. By Prof. J. A. Thomson. Melrose and Sons.

A History of the Scottish Women's Hospitals. By Eva Shaw McLaren. Hodder and Stoughton.

Vikings of To-day. By W. T. Grenfell. Marshall Bros.

Father Damien. By Edward Clifford. Macmillan.

The Life of David Livingstone. By W. G. Blakie, D.D., LL.D. John Murray.

Among the Wild Tribes of the Afghan Frontier. By Dr. Pennell. Seeley, Service.

Pennell of the Afghan Frontier. By A. M. Pennell. Seeley, Service.

Memoirs and Letters of Sir James Paget. By Stephen Paget. Longmans, Green.

Lord Lister: His Life and Work. By G. T. Wrench. Longmans, Green.

The Life of Pasteur. By René Vallery-Radot. Constable.

A Woman Doctor—Mary Murdoch of Hull. By Hope Malleson. Sidgwick and Jackson.

The Life of Sophia Jex-Blake. By Margaret Todd. Macmillan.

Sir Victor Horsley. By Stephen Paget. Constable.

At Work: Letters of Maria Elizabeth Hayes, M.D. Edited by Mrs. Hayes. S.P.G.

Pioneer Work for Women (see Bibliography, page xiv.). By Dr. Elizabeth Blackwell. Dent.

Dr. Jackson of Manchuria. By Rev. A. J. Costain, B.A. Hodder and Stoughton.

Dr. Isabel Mitchell of Manchuria. By Rev. F. W. S. O'Neill. J. Clarke.

The Way of the Good Physician. By Henry Hodgkin. L.M.S.

The Claim of Suffering. By Elma Paget. S.P.G.

Companions of My Solitude. By Sir A. Helps. George Routledge.

Friends in Council (2 vols.). By Sir A. Helps. John Murray.

Confessio Medici. Macmillan.

I Wonder. By Stephen Paget. Macmillan.

I Sometimes Think. By Stephen Paget. Macmillan.

The Corner of Harley Street: Being Some Familiar Correspondence of Peter Harding, M.D. Constable.

Living Water. By Harold Begbie. Headley Bros.

Essays on Vocation. Edited by Basil Mathews. (A second series is in course of preparation.) Oxford University Press.

Body and Soul. By Dr. Dearmer. Isaac Pitman.

Common Sense. By Dr. Jane Walker. Privately printed.

BILLING AND SONS, LTD., PRINTERS, GUILDFORD, ENGLAND

CPSIA information can be obtained
at www.ICGtesting.com
Printed in the USA
BVHW092226200922
647504BV00008B/423

9 781544 613833